What the Dreams Whisper

A Collection of Short Stories by Tween Writers

Lune Spark Books, Apex, NC

to Auntie Mary♥

Publisher: Lune Spark LLC

3651 Green Level West Rd, Apex, NC, United States

www.lunespark.com

Young Writers' Resources: www.youngwriterscontest.com

E-mail: books@lunespark.com

Phone: +1 (919) 342-0568

Ordering Information: Quantity sales. Special discounts are available on quantity purchases by corporations, associations, and others. For details, contact the publisher at the address above.

Or visit www.youngwriterscontest.com

Hardback ISBN 13: 978-1-947960-55-8

Paperback ISBN 13: 978-1-947960-54-1

eBook ISBN 13: 978-1-947960-53-4

Lune Spark Books, Apex, NC

Cover art by Trisha Rumjahn

1. Short Stories 2. Anthology 3. Creative writing 4. Young writers

First edition

"Start writing, no matter what. The water does not flow until the faucet is turned on."

- Louis L'Amour

"If I waited for perfection, I would never write a word."

- Margaret Atwood

A Collection of Short Stories by Tween Writers

Contents

Seasons of Unspoken Words..7

Colors of Loss..14

Orphanage of Colors 21

Entropy..27

You Will Sea 35

A Lotus Wish 41

Orphaned 47

Promise..54

A Rare Gift..61

A Blank Page..67

Zoo Misfits 72

Conundrum 76

Big Heart..83

A Bloody Inheritance..89

In the Depths of the Peaceful Forest..96

Countdown..99

The Purple Shell 105

Only the Purest..111

Hawaii 118

A Storm in Heaven..125

Give It a Chance *133*

The Fruit of Endurance *139*

Last Gasp *146*

Get Back Up *150*

The Book Catastrophe *156*

A Dagger from the Past *163*

This Should Not Be Scary *170*

The Myth of Medusa *177*

About Lune Spark Books *183*

Other Anthologies by Lune Spark *184*

Seasons of Unspoken Words
Zoe Chan

She loved her most in the spring.

Her graceful movements and effervescent attitude entwined with the delicate and ephemeral nature of this particular season.

The slight smile that slowly spread across her face, her petal-like lips quirking up, ever so slightly like flower buds shivering after a long winter, tentatively peeking their perianths into the buzzing air.

The way she entered a room. Her gracefulness, somehow filled with a childlike glee, was reminiscent of a baby bird as it stretched its wings, feathers trembling in the warm air as it prepared to take flight.

***

Ellie had debated, more than once, to tell her friend how she felt, but it was always like someone had forced her to swallow those words like the bitter Xanax pills that sat atop her bedside table.

Don't say it.

Because that, surely, would be a good ten years of friendship down the drain.

But it *was* tempting.

That time in summer camp. They had finished canoeing, and the sun had been starting to sink behind the rolling green hills in the distance. It had drenched everything in a warm, nostalgic kind of light, outlining everything in a hazy honey-gold.

What the Dreams Whisper

They had both been tired out from the day's activities and had been taking a quick stroll to dry themselves off and enjoy the sunset before dinner.

Ellie remembered it vividly. It had, after all, happened last summer.

"You're staring," Ari had commented.

Ellie had shook her head, her cheeks flaming redder than the red spot on Jupiter. "No, no, I just zoned out for a bit. Don't flatter yourself," she'd added dryly.

This was how her friend had remained so oblivious—Ellie had simply *refused* to show any feelings.

It was easier this way.

"Hey, Ari?" she'd blurted out before she could stop herself.

"Yeah, what?"

Ellie had struggled to form the words on the tip of her tongue. "I, um…"

But was it worth losing her friend for?

It was not.

They were best friends, first and foremost.

"Never mind," she'd whispered hoarsely, staring at the rippling lake.

***

She loved her most in the summer.

How her eyes reflected the glow of fireflies upon a meadow of viridescent green, gold scintillas among the emerald.

The plethora of freckles sprinkled here and there on her cheeks, the marks creating their own constellations that were utterly unique, so reminiscent of the stars that burned white in a pool of inky blue above.

The towering bonfire reflecting on her red-brown hair, lighting it up in shimmering shades of crimson, orange, and gold, a perfect reflection of her fiery tempest. Intoxicating, just like the burning liquor that had slid down her throat that day, filling her, all the way to her fingertips, with warmth.

***

"Oh my god, you like them, don't you?!" Ari suddenly burst out when they were eating lunch. Ellie snapped out of her trance.

"Who?" she asked, only half paying attention.

"That person, over there—blonde?" Her friend nodded in their direction. "Harper, was it? You were staring."

Ellie's face flushed slightly. No, not Harper. She was gazing at Ari, out of the corner of her eye. She was wearing a purple sweater. And Ellie had given her that same sweater. A smile curled onto her lips.

***

She loved her most in the autumn.

She had cut her brilliant flame-colored hair that fell to a sumptuous tumble to her waist short, the locks now framing her face and barely reaching her chin, achingly akin to the color-drenched maple leaves that fell gracefully onto the cobbled streets, strikingly red and orange against the gray.

Some would claim that beautiful people were the ones who stood out the most, but none of them, in Ellie's opinion, could hold a candle to Ari. She had always been comfortable fading into the background, but that was what made her stand out.

What the Dreams Whisper

How her attitude was like flipping a coin—when a group of people from the football team had laughed at Ellie for tripping during PE, Ari had become as fierce as an unexpected wind, biting at wherever she could reach. The flat side of a knife to your cheek. But after that lesson, she had been like a cup of tea by the fire, the comfort of slipping into an old sweater as she had consoled her friend.

***

And so she watched.

Watched, out of the corner of her eye, as the girl was sketching a bird perched on a tree branch. Her red-gold hair fell, a glossy, luxuriant curtain, in front of her face. Ellie itched to brush it out of the way, but her hands seemed glued to her pockets.

Watched, as Ari ranted about what had happened in the glee club she had joined last year.

Watched as the club performed, and her entire being seemed to be glowing as she stood onstage, surrounded by a halo of glowing spotlights.

Watching.

That was all she did.

Until one day, the unthinkable happened.

Well, not unthinkable. But it *was* devastating to Ellie, who watched as Ari slowly but surely succumbed to the charm of the quarterback on the football team.

And it was just her luck that said quarterback just so happened to despise her for *no* particular reason at all!

Ugh.

What a jerk, honestly. What did she see in him anyway?!

***

She loved her most in the winter.

Nobody could see it, because nobody knew her well enough. Nobody could see how her cheeks had turned up and she was smiling, laughing that laugh that sounded like a merry fire crackling during Christmas day. It was such a small thing that nobody noticed.

Nobody noticed how she had folded into herself. Everyone saw what they wanted to see—Ari, happy and laughing, cheering everyone up as she went.

Except for Ellie, who noticed her friend's change in attitude like how the leaves had slowly browned, and how frost had crept up on the roses she so loved to cultivate.

But of course—even the most beautiful of flowers don't last forever.

***

Yet, those words, those unabashed confessions of her feelings in between the lines of her scrawls, remained inked into the mound of leather-bound journals, stacking higher and higher as the months flew by like pages of a novel.

This was reminiscent of a lake. Who knew what secrets lay in the murky blue-green depths? After all, the sun only reached the surface. So much was left unsaid.

And so, the still lake teeming with unsaid thoughts remained quiet, as to not ruin anything, not cause any ripples to disturb itself any further.

After all, who falls in love with their best friend?

-

What the Dreams Whisper

"Ellie!" Ari screamed into her phone after school. "Help, help. Please, I need your help on winged eyeliner and everything else—my hands are shaking way too much, and I cannot risk looking like a cheap floozy and a half on this date!"

Ellie laughed. "Be there in five," she said lightly, successfully keeping the sadness out of her tone.

As much as it hurt, seeing the girl she had fallen for go on a date with someone else, someone who *despised* Ellie and treated her horribly, all that really mattered in the end was that Ari was happy.

Right?

"Ellie…I'm not so sure about this," Ari admitted, fiddling with the hem of her vintage purple dress. "I mean—he doesn't know me that well, and I don't know him that well either, so maybe I should just bail on this…" She trailed off. "And plus, our movie nights are probably a lot more fun anyway."

Ellie felt her heart leap in her throat. *She'd rather spend time with me.*

But she couldn't screw this up for her friend and be a mood dampener, could she?

So she plastered on a (what she hoped to be) convincing smile. "Oh, you won't know until you've tried, won't you?" she said cheerfully.

Stupid! she screamed at herself internally. There was that chance, and the precarious situation had been *perfect*—for god's sake, Ari had even said that she'd rather hang out with Ellie than the quarterback.

Rather hang out with *Ellie,* who cussed people out in British, cried over bad reality TV, hoarded candies in coat pockets—*her!*

As Ari was about to head down the hall to where her date was waiting outside, Ellie's hand shot out and grabbed her wrist. She didn't know why she did it—it was more like a visceral reaction, if anything. "Wait," she said. The words sounded foreign to her ears, as if Ellie wasn't the one saying them. "Wait, you can't go on that date," she said, stumbling over the words.

Ari tipped her head to one side, confused. Chandelier earrings dangled and sparkled. "Why not...?"

"Because he doesn't love you," Ellie whispered, looking into those viridescent emerald eyes that she could stare at for hours upon hours. "Not like I do."

Ari stared back, utter surprise on her face. She took a step back, her earrings wobbling.

"I, um—I have to go," she said, spinning around so fast that she nearly fell, before practically running down the corridor and slamming the door. The bells chimed and tinkled, leaving only the ghost of their conversation before.

And Ellie let her go.

Colors of Loss

Isabel Avrushin

Taking a tentative step forward, I shiver against the stale wind slipping against my bare arms. The waves lap over each other, sand gripping onto the surface. I taste the colors—the blues, the yellows—and the whispers of serenity, all echoing in my mind.

My brother and I have shared this spot since we were younger. Hiding from our problems, just for a little while, until it's time to face them. The best thing about this spot is that we rarely see anyone here. It's not impressive, or clean, but it's my favorite place to take in the fresh air and be with the person that understands me. I've spent most of my life in the depths of silence, a loss of communication. I live in a deaf world. At this beach, I can hear myself louder and more clearly than I ever have been able to anywhere else.

I sense the eye of the storm approaching, warning with rumbling terror that screeches through my senses. The sun surrenders to dark clouds that are jammed with forming rain. But I can't bring myself to step away from the water, clipped from the world. The brief lush of colors rush toward me as I close my eyes, taking in each second. When I open my eyes, I see him, for a moment. A flash as my brother runs into the water, under the layers of blue. I smile at his ambition. I smile until minutes go by, and still, he hasn't broken to the surface.

The air seems to get colder, tickling my spine in a breath of warning. I try to make noise, try to make him hear me. But I know he can't under the opaque froth. It makes me lose myself. Searching the waves, I can't feel the freeing sensation I had just a moment ago. Panic douses my heart, spiking with sudden fear. All I can see is gray. A drowning boat under a darkened ocean struck by lightning and thunder. It's that feeling of panic someone on that boat would feel. If it were real.

Minutes pass, second after second ticking by with no sign of my brother. It doesn't take me longer than that to realize.

My brother is gone.

***

I push my chair back with a grating scrape, the ground rumbling beneath me. I tower over my sketch made from a stick of charcoal. There are no colors in this sketch. Black lines outline and bold the face that runs away from me each passing day. It hurts to know that one day I might not know him any longer, just a distant, fogged dream. Maybe someday it will stop hurting. I hope at some point I can live my life without seeing him every second of every day. But with these minutes, this stretching time, his face turns into blotches of gray.

As I stare at my sketch, it doesn't feel right. The proportions are wrong; the smudges turn into bags instead of shadows. With the anger held in my fist, I pick up the drawing and crumble it, not being able to stare at it any longer. If I could see him, then the stars would be brighter. I would use colors to paint the world if he were here. If I weren't as lonely as I am, the world would be luminescent with hope and artistry, painted with love instead of grief. Or are they one and the same?

I grapple with the feeling of the same panic I felt the moment before I realized he was gone, all of it rushing at me. Grimly, I close my eyes, imagining myself in his position. I can feel the glazing water, even see the green, the type that reminds me of late spring, curling into the deep blues and a tad of purple. I don't move. My lungs begin screeching for air, clawing through water for something that can't be found underneath. I stay there for a minute longer until I pull myself back to my body, gasping for air.

That's what happened to my brother.

***

"Your brother isn't an excuse for why you don't communicate with anyone," my dad signs, his lips moving at the same time with the words that are muted from me.

How do you expect me to communicate with anyone when they can't understand me? I sign back with fury.

"You had more friends when your brother was here; you're lonely," he says.

That's because he was my translator, and also my best friend. Now I don't have either.

"You shouldn't rely on other people for your life."

Do you think I have a choice?

"I think you should start living for yourself."

I stomp my foot, glaring at him.

"Don't give me that look."

My insides burn with the anger that consumes my thoughts. Instead of willing myself to stand here, watching him as he looks down on me for the losses I've pushed away, I run out the door, not looking behind me.

***

I'm here again, his smile in the front of my mind. But this time, watching the waves construct a breath of earth, I fall onto the sand. And in a way, I can feel his colors pooling into the palms of my hands that I press into the ground. I can feel my brother's golden hue reaching for the sky, straight from the sun, the moon, the stars. His smile was silver outlined in gold. I had almost forgotten the light feeling behind his grin, but remembering it now hurts me more than ever.

My breath quickens with the waves as I gulp down and blink back tears, holding back, containing every feeling within me.

What the Dreams Whisper

I stand back up, staring out at the horizon. The world is silent, but I can see the way it calls with the wind that twines with the waves, slate with gloomy arsenic. I try to dip a foot into the blue, cold already shivering up the flesh of my toes when at an inch away. I flinch back before I can touch the water.

I'm afraid. But more than afraid. I'm afraid that I can never feel the colors again. I'm afraid that I will hold everything within me. Afraid because I'm hiding from the world. Standing here, watching the sky collapse and cave into the waters, folding and molding, compacting together, I breathe in, holding my breath until my lungs screech for air. When I let loose my breath, I see him standing before me.

My brother begins fading away within a matter of seconds. He reaches out, and I mirror his movement, outstretching my hand for the fading silhouette. In the seconds before we touch, he vanishes completely, leaving me to stand here, still reaching for the ghost that's left me wondering if I'm going insane.

I hold my hand close to my chest, his final breath sifting through the air. I stare after him, but there's nothing left. I'm beginning to think I've lost my mind.

*****

Our house is packed with family and friends, a gathering to celebrate the life of my brother. Barely anyone here understands me, or who I am. I'm just the poor sister to take pity on. Everywhere I go, there's someone crying or looking like they're on the brink of letting tears fall. So I push my way through to the door, feeling at loss of air. I make it outside, and the refreshing cool of spring hits me instantly. I collapse on the back porch stairs, closing my eyes to hold back all the emotions that swarm my head all at once. For the first time, I fear hearing myself. I don't open my eyes, even as I feel the thud next to me as someone sits down.

I don't want to talk to anyone, but someone taps my shoulder and I have no choice but to breathe in my irritation and open my eyes to the gaze of my father.

He begins to say something, but hesitates. And then he both signs and mouths, "Are you going to be okay?"

I don't realize I'm crying until I taste the salty solution of tears in my mouth. I clench my fists to keep from trembling or letting out an unwanted sob.

Quickly, I wipe away my tears, but more come anyway. I can feel my dad's gaze as he doesn't know what to do.

I shake my head. *I don't know,* I sign. My dad sits next to me as I sob uncontrollably. Because I don't know if I'm going to be okay. I don't know what I'm going to do, or what I want to do. And each moment that I realize I'm losing track of my life it hurts even more because my brother isn't going to be here to help me. I look over to my dad, and he may be nothing like my brother, but he is the only person I have left. And then I notice the small tear escaping from his eye.

What the Dreams Whisper

"Neither do I," he signs. And I'm crying harder, but this time it's not because everything hurts. This time it's because I don't feel as alone as I thought I was.

Orphanage of Colors
Fiza Faisal

Yara scowled as she saw the neighborhood children bracing for another try. A small boy with beautiful curls tentatively walked to the gate, putting one foot before the next. His jaw quivered and he ran back with a whimper. Ayda rolled her eyes. "My turn!" she cried, and sprinted to the gate of the dilapidated house. She gripped the bars firmly in her small hands, counted to ten breathlessly, and raced back. "And that's how you do it," she announced with a proud look on her face. "You should not give Old Lucy the time to start controlling you."

"There's no ghost in that little house," said Yara. "I bet you there isn't anything or anyone there, and hasn't been for years."

"If you're so confident, why don't you go check it out yourself?" asked Ayda. "I will accept it if you come out alive and sane."

They glared at each other for a while. Finally, Yara broke the silence.

"Fine," she snapped. "I'll go."

Under her friends' curious gazes, Yara walked up to the gate, pulled the rusty lock up, and pushed until it creaked open. The wooden boards that the house was built with were a dark, faded purple. The glass on the windows was streaked with dirt. The door was a yellow shade that had peeled in places, giving way to the brown of the wood underneath.

Yara pushed on the aged wood, and it yielded immediately. A smell, of all things old, unkempt, and uncared for, hit her, and she shuddered. She stepped in.

It seemed to be a living room. Cobwebs lined the corners from floor to ceiling. On a windowsill was a cracked flowerpot with long-rotten, bent flowers in it. The floor was a palimpsest of dust that had collected on it in layers. Yara did not want to disturb it, yet she had to take a light step.

A cloud flew up into the air. Yara sneezed hard. She looked around in fright, but everything was as before. So she was right, she thought, there was nobody here after all.

Yara walked along a corridor, past an old closed door to her left, into a dining room with a table and two chairs in the middle. Maybe, somebody had lived here before. Then she noticed the tabletop.

It had to be the cleanest thing in the house. There was a stack of papers on it. A few of the sheets were old and brown at the edges. Yara picked one from the top and started reading:

Dear William,

Today I thought of you as I baked some chocolate cake. You have always loved my cakes. We used to joke that the only reason you would marry me were those dark chocolate brownies.

Do you remember the evenings you walked into my bakery to the sweet smell of vanilla and warm bread? We were so young. And the night we shared our first slice of cake together? Warm rich chocolate in our mouths, creamy eloquence of violin in our ears.

And do you remember the time you first kissed me? You said my lips tasted like chocolate, William, but it was a violet kiss to me. As violet as the tulips you wore in your breast pocket that day. As violet as the neon lamp that reflected off your kind eyes.

The day I baked my first red velvet. You caressed the traces of carmine batter on my finger as you slipped the ring onto it. The ring! I lost it. Is it the guilt that weighs me down? I must find it before you return.

Did you recognize this gorgeous blue ink? It is your favorite fountain pen. I chided you for forgetting it everywhere. Remember the time you left it on your chair at that wedding? God bless Ezra for finding it before we left!

Our Ezra was wonderful today. As adorable as ever, in her favorite brown shirt and little blue pinafore. My little angel! She measured the flour and sugar for me, and helped me lift the hot pan. Sometimes, my mind is not as sharp as I would like it to be, and I am not able to remember my recipes.

Wick knocked my coffee over this morning. However many times Ezra apologized for that little dog, I cannot recall! I dried the coffee off that little note that you sent me, William. I do not remember receiving it. Is it silly that I miss you so much?

I still have the music you had written for me so long ago. Do you recollect how I first used to laugh at your compositions? But they became the most beautiful in the world, William. Those hours were the best of my life.

Your notes traveling from my bow, wafting in the wind as the scent of freshly baked bread. Oh, the colors I saw in your music! The deep crescendos, wavering melodies, merging in perfect harmony until my fingers moved without my willing

What the Dreams Whisper

them. And clear to me through all that, your hand beating out the steady rhythm on your armchair. Your hand, that was gentle and firm, like worn denim. Do you remember how we danced together that night, you and I? I know you remember. Neither of us could ever forget. The cool breeze hitting our faces, your dark eyes brilliant in the haze of night, as if all the light stolen from the stars before it hit the earth was directed onto your face. Your obscure black eyes, impenetrable to anyone but me. That slight curve of your lips that nobody notices.

I see you in everything, William. I see you in the beautiful violet tulips at the windows, in the glorious sunrises and sunsets that we had welcomed together, which I now yearn for alone. I see you in Ezra's smile and Wick's prance. I know she misses you as dearly as I do. Do return to us soon.

Love,

Farah

Who were these people? Who was Ezra? Yara had never seen her playing outside with the other pesky kids. She compulsively arranged the stack of papers, and as she did so, a withered sheet with a hurried scrawl fell out.

27 of April, 1945

My dear Farah,

If all goes well, we can welcome the new year together. Please have some cake ready for me. I shall try my best to smuggle you some of the *Schokolade* that they give here. It is delicious.

Kisses,

William

Yara felt a sudden urge to open that door that she had left closed. She walked across and nudged it open gently. The room had two windows on each side, each with rotten flowers similar to the ones Yara had seen in the living room. A beautiful doll with curly black tresses sat in a corner with a dappled stuffed puppy on its lap. Its clothes were torn and faded—a brown shirt and a blue jumper.

Yara almost shrieked as she saw what was in the middle of the room. Two armchairs were placed there. In one of them sat...Old Lucy?

It was an old woman holding a violin in her wrinkled arms, her eyes closed, her face scrunched into a smile. Her bow began to move tardily over the strings, and music started spreading through the room. It was light but melancholy, bittersweet, like dark chocolate. Yara's heart rose and fell with the music as it swelled and shrunk and faded as wisps.

Yara stepped closer, her arm involuntarily stretching toward the stooped shoulder. Just then, the music stopped, and the woman started murmuring. Smothering her fear, Yara leaned closer, till she could hear:

"Mix and crumble. Mix and crumble..."

"I mix in the sugar. Mix and crumble..."

"You will love it...just a little milk...mix and add more..."

"You have always loved my chocolate fudge..."

Her lips were barely moving, her eyes were glazed. Yara took one last look at the woman who seemed oblivious to her presence. As Yara turned, she caught sight of the dusty plaque next to the doll. The rims of the plaque were gold, the writing engraved in gray.

William Abdel

1920–1945

For Valiant and Dedicated Service

Yara froze. She stood there for a few minutes, waiting for the music that did not start again. She felt bare, and a weight settled on her shoulders. She gently stepped out and shut the door.

Yara stumbled to the front door and pulled it open. Beyond the gate, she recognized terror and admiration on Ayda's face.

Words rushed out of her mind, but faltered before she could speak.

"This…is a ghost house. It is a house of memories. An orphanage of colors. Colors lived here, laughing, crying, and longing, even after the world became impervious to them. Ghosts, unborn, undead, who had stayed on and kept each other alive, long after they were supposed to have faded away."

She just smiled.

Entropy
Hannah Kwan

Fear. That seemed to be the only emotion left in the world.

Calla pushed herself up and jumped off her mattress. A ting of metal filled the air. She gazed up at what used to be summer sky and frowned. She remembered having to squint at the sun to keep from being blinded by light. It had been replaced by the heavy, gray clouds that loomed over the earth like deep-sea scavengers, watching people's every move. The people who remembered the nuclear war had seen them crackle with ice-blue rays at night. But now, they swirled slowly, tired and resentful. The clouds haunted them.

Calla forced herself up and walked over to the doorway of the girls' dorm. Two soldiers stood solemnly by both sides, their arms stiff in their new-old black overcoats. She glanced at them: prewar wools, from the clothes-recycling factory.

"Two minutes left for water collection. You're late." One typed her attendance into his plasticky smartphone.

"I know, and I don't want to be reminded," she spat, rushing out into the rye fields and over to the well where everybody else was lined up. Most then milled around in the food market by its side.

She pushed through the crowd, quickly drawing a bucket of water from the well. She ignored the scowling guards on either side, irritated that she was late. She took one glance at their rifles, collected her food and medicine rations, and disappeared into the dwindling crowd; a key skill in this world. She was eager to never be on the receiving ends of the soldiers' weapons.

A few other guards had already begun cleaning up.

With a tired grunt, a filthy army ration truck charged through the fields, rushing toward the crowd at unbelievable speed.

The truck slammed into the food carts, sending one flying in the air and hurtling toward the screaming crowd—

Calla watched as a scrambling young boy tripped and landed on the ground with a thud, sealing his fate. His face, twisted with fear, could be seen for a brief moment before the food cart landed on his struggling body, committing a brutal murder.

The soldiers lifted the cart to find the boy's body, pale as bone. The crowd settled, cowed, and stood in brooding silence, still and motionless as the boy himself. Calla stared into his cold, lifeless eyes with dread.

Wisps of white smoke emerged from the boy's body, rising into the air. Panic seized Calla as the smoke gradually solidified. She toppled to the ground, shaking with anguish.

A figure resembling the boy began to form, his features growing increasingly visible. Large, fearful eyes stared back at Calla with dismay. His thin figure was covered in cuts and bruises that bled a dark, inky liquid. It slid down his thigh, gushing out of the wounds down his back, staining his shirt a horrid shade of obsidian black.

The boy lifted his hands and looked at himself. What used to be his flesh was now pale, almost transparent, like water clouded with dust—

"What are you doing lying there, kid?" a soldier questioned, clutching Calla by her furry coat's lapel and pulling her off the ground. He was missing a finger.

Calla looked around to find everyone either speaking in hushed tones, chewing the soldiers out about the accident, or weeping with despair.

It was as if they hadn't seen a thing.

"There's nothing to see here. Move on," the soldier ordered.

"But—the ghost! The boy—a ghost—appeared—" Calla stammered, the words refusing to form.

The soldier sighed and put her down. "You're in shock. Let's go—"

"No—not the hospital!" Calla shouted, struggling from the soldier's grip. "You have to listen to me! We've all heard of special people who can—"

The soldier's expression was clouded with concern. His voice softened, but he steered Calla toward his commanding officer.

***

"A hallucination, sir… ghosts… radiation… chromosomal?"

"Stop a public panic…"

Calla sat at the edge of her hospital bed, fuming. The muffled voices of government officials and hospital staff were beginning to test her patience. The bedsheets scratched lightly at her fingers.

The hospital was a nightmare. White mattresses, sheets, and metal bars overlapped like an abstract painting. The room reeked of disinfectant.

"Do you need any help, dear?" a nurse asked, her sugary voice and radiant smile almost mocking Calla.

She shook her head. Speech was getting harder.

In an often unsmiling society, the nurses' honeyed voices and forced smiles seemed like vultures imitating the grace and elegance of peacocks. Their words were long, slow, and broken, as if Calla needed help understanding English.

An IV drip dangled from Calla's arm. A cluster of tubes and tape sank their teeth into her. The doctor wouldn't say why.

She was alone, too. It had been a week since she'd seen anybody other than the staff and other patients. "Visiting hours are over," they always said. Calla had begun to question if the visiting hours existed at all. Just like she'd heard, the hospital was a prison. A cage, where allegedly sinister people were hidden and locked up. Where were her friends? Where was her family? Or, at least, what was left of it?

The double doors of the hospital burst open, and five figures strode into the room.

"Stop right there!" a soldier cried, pointing an accusing finger at the nurse behind Calla. She dropped the IV and stepped away from the bed.

The five figures approached Calla, circling her bed at a safe distance away from her, as if she would bite if they came too close.

Two soldiers. A Transitional Military Administration boss.

Gold tab—regional, Calla noted.

A doctor hunched at his side with the head nurse.

"Please, sir. She's resting," the doctor pleaded.

The official ignored him, scowling at Calla. "You saw a ghost?"

"It was a hallucination, sir. Please," the doctor protested.

"She was traumatized," the nurse added.

Calla hissed with frustration. "It wasn't a hallucination. We've all heard of more and more people seeing—souls—" she exclaimed, trying to find a less suspicious word.

Silence fell over the room. She felt everybody's eyes burn into her.

Then the boss turned to his men and murmured.

"Isolate…"

The soldiers held her down on her bed.

The head nurse reached for a syringe and hesitantly injected Calla. She gasped, head falling back on her strawy pillow as she slipped out of consciousness.

***

Darkness. Calla could only see darkness.

Slowly, she forced her eyes open, squinting. A dim light. Cell. The door… Where was the door? She tried to turn, before looking down to find herself secured to a chair, her wrists and ankles cuffed, her arms tied to the back.

She could hear faint voices coming from the door behind her.

"Local prevalence of mutations…" a gravelly voice muttered.

That's what the army thinks: radioactive fallout is causing mutations.

The voices alternated between angry buzzing and cowed whispering.

***

Calla lay half asleep.

Tap, tap, tap.

Taps like a cockroach, by her side in the darkness. Opening one red, watery eye, she fixated on a white-gloved hand, tapping things out of a jar by her side.

Exhausted, she fell asleep again, running hand in hand through gray clouds with the boy.

***

Calla was pricked awake by a bite on her foot. A fire ant. They'd survived the war. *Better than us.* Unlike humans, their soldiers hadn't become society's queens. The sting pierced the fog in her mind, and voices outside came into focus.

"Local prevalence of visions…" the first voice murmured. "Antipsychotic dosage…"

Calla froze. She strangled a moan and a shiver. The steps grew closer, echoing on the concrete walls outside.

She closed her eyes. Being seen awake never made things better anymore.

But then the steps took an abrupt turn right. Another corridor.

"More in the regional rations…"

Not me. The Administration was drugging their town's food rations. Her friends' pale faces flashed in her mind. What else were they putting into rations? What were they controlling?

"What have they done?" Calla croaked, tears spilling from her eyes, warm as they slid down her cheeks. "What have they done to this world?"

She stared at her body, tied against the wooden chair. She stared at the dull, stone walls of her cell. She watched in silence as her tears landed on the stone slabs.

And do they have no choice?

***

An inky darkness flooded the walls as they seemed to cave in and grow smaller, as if the edges of her perception were burning and coiling like dead leaves. The dusky little lightbulb illuminated her, strapped to her chair, arms behind her back.

Softness. A warm little arm draped itself across her shoulders. She opened her eyes. The ghost of the young boy stood by her side and smiled back at her.

He had to be no older than seven. Yet, peering into his large gray eyes, they held sadness that some took a lifetime to learn.

He was no longer bleeding. His clothes were stained with the loathsome black liquid. His limbs were covered in long gray scars, like streams of tears. A menacing scar was slashed across his lips. Even so, he smiled at Calla.

He wrapped his arms around her, holding her as she fought back tears. He was frail, but the boy held her with the strength she had lost along the way.

"It's all right," he whispered.

It was as if she was a child again.

Calla cried silently into the boy's arms, holding on to her final embrace.

She would grow old and weary in this cell, and watch the rest of the world crumble, entropically, like nebulae. She would rely on the company of the ghost until it left this world, leaving her in the twilight of her life, helpless and alone.

You Will Sea
Natalie Pidgeon

Chloe Marshall was a very intelligent fourth-grader who lived in Breckenridge, Colorado, born and raised. She was a mountain girl true to the heart, so when her parents announced they were taking their first ever tropical vacation to the coast of Belize she wasn't exactly turning cartwheels.

As the plane wheels screeched to a stop, the intercom erupted and the pilot said, "Welcome to Belize, local time 12:32 p.m. The weather is eight-five degrees and sunny. I hope you enjoyed your flight and thank you for flying with us!"

Chloe wasn't quite as enthusiastic as the pilot. As the Marshalls piled off the plane, trudging down the steps, they were enveloped in a rush of warm air and humidity.

"This is really a change from the twenty-three degree Fahrenheit weather back home," Dad exclaimed.

Mom laughed, and five-year-old Clara was practically exploding with excitement as they headed toward the pier.

The water taxi to Caye Caulker was uneventful even though the captain told them it was "*UnBelizeable.*" To Chloe it didn't seem so amazing. The dusty streets of Caye Caulker were jam-packed with pedestrians, and it felt like the buildings lining the road were only getting tighter. The upcoming houseboat trip was looming in Chloe's mind, and her phobia of the ocean was all she could think about. Chloe wondered if she was the only one who didn't want to get salt water in her eyes, who was scared of the dangerous monsters that lurked beneath the depths of the water, and who noticed that all of the animals just went to the bathroom right in the sea!

That evening after checking into their thatched bungalow for one night they walked to an oceanfront restaurant called Wild Mango.

"This is going to be such authentic seafood, right on the beach!" Mom exclaimed.

"Well said," replied Dad.

Clara meanwhile was studying the menu intently.

"Can I have this?" She pointed to an entree called Squid + Shrimp Salad.

"Sure, sweetie," Dad confirmed. Chloe grimaced.

"What about you, honey?" Mom asked Chloe.

"I'll stay safe with fish fingers," Chloe replied.

Once they had ordered their seafood, Chloe took a moment to look around. Mounted on the wall were various sea creatures. A purple miniature octopus was dramatically posed, and its black eyes made Chloe squirm. Several starfish were pinned to the wall, and their nonexistent eyes looked straight through Chloe's skull. Last and most frightening was the deadly lionfish. Chloe looked away in horror to continue picking at her fish fingers.

***

The next morning with the water around the houseboat churning from the engines the Captain shouted, "Welcome aboard the *Streamline Sea Lion.*"

No turning back now, thought Chloe. The houseboat was all theirs for one night and two days. It would stop at various places to snorkel, kayak, and beach comb.

"Who's ready to snorkel?!" Dad said enthusiastically.

"I want to see a big shark!" Clara cried.

"Maybe," said Mom.

Chloe popped on a neon-orange life vest and put her snorkel mask on her forehead. Her heart was thumping out of her chest. Panic froze her as she sat down on the edge of the boat. Meanwhile, Clara accidentally toppled into the water.

"The water's warm," Clara remarked.

Then Dad dove in beside Clara. He playfully tugged on Chloe's left ankle, and she lost her grip and belly flopped into the sea.

Chloe rose to the surface and coughed out a mouthful of seawater. By that time Mom had slipped into the water, graceful as ever, and Clara was already off. Mom kicked off behind Clara, and Chloe followed them. A gurgling sensation arose in Chloe's stomach, knowing that she was drifting in a sea creature toilet.

They saw so many ocean creatures that day: a moray eel (Clara tried to touch the eel); a hawksbill turtle; an eagle ray; a nurse shark (Clara was happy about that, but when the shark dove at her aggressively because she tried to ride it, her opinion changed); a lionfish (Chloe's swim back to the *Streamline Sea Lion* was Olympic speed). Clara was amazed by these sea creatures and wanted to go again.

That evening, Dad said, "It's almost nightfall, girls. Mom is helping the captain fix us dinner. So for now just hang out and read a book."

To Chloe those were the best words ever spoken, but to Clara not so much! Chloe settled into her book, *The Adventures of Doctor Dolittle*. Fatigue overtook her and she fell into a deep sleep.

No one bothered to wake her up for dinner, so when she awoke in the morning before everyone else, she was famished. She tried to shake awake Clara, who was murmuring in her sleep, "But the hot dog ate the chicken and my magnifying glass." No use, thought Chloe. She made her way to the kitchen where she found a banana. She peeled it and ate it in three gulps.

"Much better," said Chloe.

In ten minutes, everyone was awake because Clara had accidentally sleepwalked into a shelf full of pans and knocked them down.

Dad made breakfast (calamari chowder). Clara inhaled the calamari chowder in a few mouthfuls.

"Can we make oatmeal like this at home?" inquired Clara.

Dad chuckled.

"Chloe, you haven't touched your chowder," said mom.

"I'd prefer a piece of toast," replied Chloe.

At Chloe's request, Mom arose to butter a piece of toast.

Relief swept over Chloe as she bit into the toast.

"We should go kayaking this morning," Dad said.

***

After breakfast the Marshall family put on their swimsuits and prepared for an adventure. The captain said today would be a good day to go kayaking because the ocean was calm. They anchored the boat in the sand near a coral reef. The captain explained that as the land got higher and came level with the reef, the water from the deep ocean would break over the shallow reef and create waves.

Dad got in a green kayak first, and Mom slipped in a narrow purple kayak. Clara scrambled into a small bright-orange kayak while Chloe sat down in a pink one.

Once the fear inside Chloe's chest faded she realized this activity was quite fun. As far as Chloe could see, the only skills involved were laughing and having fun.

The captain attached ropes to each of their kayaks and then tied them to the boat. He towed them out to the edge of the reef, where they were untied and the waves pushed them back toward the reef. This was the most fun Chloe had had in a long time. She smiled in a satisfied way.

After lunch (fish sandwiches) it was time for "the last adventure of the day" (as Dad would say). As if on cue, Dad said, "Adventure number three, last but not least."

Beachcombing was the very last activity they would be doing on the *Streamline Sea Lion*. The captain anchored the boat a few feet from the beach. As everyone jumped off the boat, they were surprised to find that their feet could touch the bottom easily. The coarse sand felt like a massage on Chloe's dry feet. They walked to the beach. It was coated in multicolored seashells as far as the eye could see. Clara bent down and picked up a conch shell. The outside was brown, and algae clung to the shell. But the inside was a brilliant pink that was smooth and shiny. Clara held it up to her ear and was in awe that she could hear the ocean in it. Chloe saw a glimmer in the distance. She ran toward the spot and picked up a spiral shell that was spangled with red and white. After studying it, she shoved it in her prized seashell satchel. Chloe also found a beautiful (but brittle) sand dollar that crumbled in her fingers.

After everyone had collected an array of unique seashells, they headed back to the houseboat. Chloe sat alone on the top bunk in the cabin of the houseboat thinking. She realized that all the fears that had been nagging her meant nothing. They were holding her back from doing what she loved—exploring the natural world around her.

Without even asking permission, she grabbed her snorkel, mask, and fins then dove straight into the water, clothes and all. Chloe kicked with joy. She thought nothing of her long-gone fears as she finally got to appreciate the beauty of the ocean. She marveled at needlefish and gazed in awe at a sleeping eel hidden beneath a cove of rocks. She smiled at a sea anemone saying hello in the waves among beautiful beds of coral.

Something warm and fuzzy rose in her chest. She felt happier than she had ever been before. To Chloe, contentment was the best feeling of all. As she resurfaced, the world seemed brighter. From that day on, whenever possible, Chloe would try new things and have a positive attitude about unfamiliar and different ideas always and forever.

A Lotus Wish

Ziheng Shen

Every story starts out like a flower, and every flower has a story. They spread and grow, in the ground, taking in water. They can grow when spring offers rain and can continue to grow until they meet their death, flourishing until the end.

One thing that humans and flowers have in common: we always know when to face the sun when things go wrong.

Humans are never invincible when harsh words come into play. We often shed tears quietly by ourselves.

That is where our story begins…

***

"Nina? Where've you gone this time?"

I glanced up from my journal. My mom was a kind woman with dark hair, caring brown eyes, and a smile that seemed to never go away. Except for the times when she got angry—then things could get rough with her. She never let a question go without an answer. She was our general, and we were her soldiers.

"I'M NOT HOME!" my younger sister Nina called from the backyard.

"Well, of course you're not." My mother walked over to the sliding glass door in the back of the house, her shoulders tense. "You're currently outside without my saying so— WHAT ARE YOU DOING?"

I giggled as I watched my mother run outside, anger written on her face. From just looking at her expression, I

What the Dreams Whisper

could tell that she figured out where my sister was, outside where she was obviously rolling in the mud with our dog Tussle.

Tussle was a cute border collie, and we found him when I was just eight. Now I'm eleven, and my sister is seven. My sister and I had found Tussle when we were playing hide-and-seek. He was shivering in the cold, extremely damp, and his fur was all matted and he was missing a patch of fur.

Just the thought of that picture gave me shivers down my spine.

I heard my sister scream her high-pitched scream, and I laughed even more. She will never understand that we have limits, like everyone else.

I bent down to continue writing in my journal, excitement bubbling up for the upcoming competition.

***

It was time for the competition. As I stepped onto the course with Tussle, I smiled, because I knew that we were gonna win it. We started, nailing the jumps, gliding through with efficiency, and coming to the end with a record time. Of course, that was expected because Tussle and I had won this race five years in a row!

As we finished, Nina came over and knelt down to scratch Tussle behind the ears. He licked Nina's hand affectionately, and we both smiled.

"I wish that I could have my *own* pet someday," she whispered, eyes shining.

"What did I say about owning another pet?" My mother glared down at her.

"Oops," she whispered to me. The she turned and started running.

My sister really was something.

***

I grabbed my purple journal from the marble counter and put on my jacket since it was still pretty cold outside. Then I opened the door and ran down to the lake I usually went to. I called it the Lotus Lake. It was named that since this lake had lotuses growing in it, and there were lily pads and other stuff too, making me love it so much that I just had to name it. I sat down on the big rock that was right next to the lake and grabbed my journal.

But as I stared at it, I realized that I had no idea what to write. So instead, I just stared at the flowers, at the lake, and at nature's beauty. The lake seemed undisturbed, just rippling a bit, making it seem like a big mirror on the ground, mirroring everything that it could catch. The lotuses were like big cups with pink edges and leaves that seemed like plates for the flowers.

I watched the lake all day—it seemed like forever. Then I went home to sleep.

***

My mom never let me go to parties. But when my friend gave me an invitation to her party, I just had to go. I planned out what I was going to say to my mother, then I explained my situation to her. I watched my mother's expression every time I took a pause for breath, and I realized that she really was listening intently. When I finally finished, I stayed quiet, waiting for something.

Then my mother said in her best unquivering voice, "I—I understand that you want to go, but—"

What the Dreams Whisper

Another voice interrupted her. "C'mon, just let her go. I mean, she's never been to one in all her life while her friends have. Let her go just this once?"

My mother and I turned to face my father, who was right behind me. He put a hand on my shoulder, making me feel protected, loved.

My mother nodded, but I could tell she did not want me to go.

***

I don't remember much about the night of the party, but I do remember is this. When I was about to leave, I noticed my mother swaying and she held on to my dad for support. She looked weak and pale, not like how she usually did.

Just the sight of her made me remember the one time when I almost fell down the stairs, and her pale face looked so frightened.

I said my goodbyes to my mother and father and left for the party, head down with guilt that I couldn't quite explain.

***

A river streamed down my face as I rushed over to the Lotus Lake. I stumbled and fell, which suddenly made my world turn upside down. Everything I saw was blurry, and before I knew it, I was on my back, sobbing near the lake.

Everything that had happened in the past few weeks had happened too quickly for me to see the signs of my mother in her weak state.

Now, I had lost her, and there was nothing I could do about it.

A few days ago, the hospital had called to tell us that she had passed away in her sleep.

I wiped my tears away angrily, wondering how it was possible to be so careless about my family.

I sighed, grabbed a photo out of my pocket, and observed every inch of it.

There was my sister and father, and myself, of course, and last but not least was my mother. She looked healthy, great, and in shape. Now, I would never see her again, and I would never get the chance to say goodbye.

"WHY?" I screamed into the depths of the lake.

***

It was my fault, my fault, MY FAULT! My mother had died, and now my sister would too? Would I lose my sister?

Not long ago, she was diagnosed with a rare dangerous disease, and now she's sick.

Emotions overwhelmed me, like a gigantic wave, just swallowing me up.

As I stared blankly at the lotuses, a thought started in my head, and I whispered, "Please, please. I beg you. Don't take my sister away. Please."

I made a wish, my first ever wish in my entire life, and I clung to it.

***

I saw a light, coming through from the dark clouds. It seemed to tell me: *Don't give up. Look for the bright side of things.* I rushed outside, and there, on the pavement, lay a golden bracelet. It shined as if brand-new, and as I picked it up, the bracelet seemed to hum in my hands. Right there, in the middle, was the picture of a *lotus*.

I held on to it. What if it healed my sister?

What the Dreams Whisper

***

It was time to celebrate. My sister was healed, completely. The lake was still, like it always was, and there, in the middle, were the cuplike lotuses with their beautiful pink edges. I smiled, my smile growing wider as I looked on longer at the beautiful flowers. The sunlight glowed, warming my face.

"Thank you," I whispered, grabbing the golden bracelet from my pocket.

I could make out a shape in the clouds.

My mother.

And suddenly, I knew that everything was going to be okay, and my family would never, ever break again.

***

Every story ends like a flower, and every flower ends like a story.

Orphaned
Kiana Shah

Hong Kong, 1945.

Clutching a dusty sack of stolen flatbreads, I shuffled along a bombed-out street. Craters gaped at me from every side, as if howling alongside the approaching typhoon, and buildings had been reduced to charred skeletons by Allied bombing raids. The city's years of misery were written in our faces, but we weren't without hope.

"Ezmia," yelled Alice, my only friend. We were street children. Our orphanage had collapsed in a fire. There was panic in her hazel eyes that I didn't see often. "Something's falling—!"

I looked up, and sure enough, from the jagged top corner of a dignified white stone building at our side, a sharp block dived off, screaming toward us like a banshee in the wind.

I made a run for it, scraping a raw ankle on the rubble-strewn ground. I was used to it. When I got to Alice, intact, but pale, with some scrapes and bruises, her eyes were stretched bigger than I realized eyes could stretch.

I interrogated her between hoarse breaths. "Why are you so surprised?"

"Did you see how fast you ran?" Alice asked. We were both finally regaining some sense. "You looked blurry."

"We're hallucinating. It's not the first time we have. We're starving and sunburned," I croaked wearily.

She shrugged. As usual, my sensible friend was focusing on the real challenge. "Where shall we get our next meal now?" Alice asked, gesturing to the piece of debris that was now covering our sack.

"We're around Central. Look around?" I proposed.

My eye caught an antique shop along the road ahead, somehow still in business. I saw our faces in an old mirror. I was covered in grime, and my dark gray eyes looked puffier than the last time I checked. My used-to-be-shoulder-length brown hair was now approaching my hips, dry and ragged at the tips, and streaked with grime, like a forest nymph.

There was suddenly a sharp pain in my body, like lightning coursing through my veins. It went away as quickly as it came, but I knew it was there. And I recognized it…

***

Alice and I were walking through a Sheung Wan alley, searching for some food. Hope embraced us like a guardian angel. We slid our eyes as we passed stalls and suits, expecting to find something to steal or grab. Bowler-hatted men smoked pipes and children played with much-polished toys, enjoying a lull in the storm.

We came across a boy at a stall laden with stale bread.

"Alice," I whispered, careful not to cause a scene, and nodded toward him.

"We need a plan." Alice said, already pondering.

"I'll circle behind to grab," I suggested, already making my way toward the boy. "But you have to be ready with a sack."

"Fine." She sighed, drawing out the word.

My half-dressed feet padded through the crowd, on the wet cobblestones.

His tired eyes roved mindlessly.

That is one thing I learned from years of stealing stuff—if you act like you belonged there, nobody will question you.

I sneaked up to grab a piece, when I noticed a patrol of Japanese soldiers, making their way toward us. I cursed under my breath and backed off. The sun, now emerging from clouds and shining on me, likewise glinted on the metal ends of their rifles. I suddenly became very still, my hand reached out amid the bodies.

Then I realized the soldiers had their eyes focused on the boy, not me.

Malevolence gripped me. The soldiers—*they're* the robbers that leave us no choice but to steal. *They're* the reason I lost my family. *They're* the reason we starve.

The more I thought about all the things they did to us, the more I wanted to stop them. I knew I would. Everyone had caught sight of the soldiers. Including the boy they were focused on.

All my hatred, from years of oppression, knotted and churned in my chest. My instincts guided me. My thieving hand balled up into a fist, and I imagined the soldiers' heads, gashed open on the alley's walls.

That is exactly what happened. Their bodies floated, like angels, for just a moment.

And they flew, limbs flying like ragdolls, into the wall.

Blood flowed down it and pooled at its bottom.

The crowd crumpled with terror.

In the chaos, I grabbed some bread and ran for Alice, my heart pumping with an otherworldly strength.

***

When we were a safe distance away, Alice burst with glee. She was so excited that some of the soldiers were defeated, she was rambling on about the afternoon. Sadism wasn't in her nature. But nobody wanted the Japanese here.

"They just floated off the ground, like something was controlling them. And after that, everyone was *completely* silent…"

That moment, it felt as though lightning shot through my body, and I yelped in pain, catching Alice's attention.

"What happened? Are you all right?" she asked, suddenly concerned about me.

But I wasn't. I had felt that sensation before today.

My mind was filled with the image of that piece of rubble, plummeting toward me. Abruptly, I stood upright, an idea coming to mind.

"Alice," I whispered, almost as if I was scared of what I was going to say. "I think I…"

A split second after the words left my mouth, an *incredibly* loud siren rang through my ears, as if a fox was howling at me, just ten million times louder.

Alice and I shared a look—our big eyes shined with hollow hopefulness. *A bombing raid.*

Just then, there was a roar and a heat wave—the building next to us caught fire, burning my eyes. It buckled and groaned, and rubble fell toward our heads, the threat of death looming above us.

This time, I knew I couldn't run. The building was falling too fast. I stood there and let the building take me.

I would be dead. I would never be able to see my parents again. Never able to say bye to my only friend.

Never. Never. Never, screaming in my head, like a mantra.

But when I woke up…

I was still lying on the same charred ground I had been when the building caught fire. Alice was still beside me. I couldn't understand why I was alive. I was supposed to be dead.

I looked up, and saw a milky-white light, shrouding us as if in a bubble. The world beyond it was a blur of gray skies and the burned skeletons of the city's buildings.

Maybe this was heaven.

But I didn't think it was. It was just as gloomy as it had been before. I was still starving, maybe even a little more. And my body screamed with pain, as if every cell had burned with lightning.

Then, I realized it. I had powers. I could protect myself.

And with that realization, promptly, I fainted.

***

"Finally, she's awake," a teasing voice said as my eyes fluttered open. "You've been out for a few hours."

I looked up, and there was Alice. A miracle. She was alive. I immediately felt tears coming to my parched eyes and tried to hold them back.

"Where are we?"

We were in what seemed to be a stone cottage, with shelves lining the walls. There were bottles with chemicals, dried eyeballs from various animals, and leather-bound textbooks. I was lying on a bed with a metal frame and beige sheets covering me. Only the pots of mysterious dried powders felt like Hong Kong.

"You are in my house," said a beautiful woman behind Alice.

I had not noticed her before that moment. She was wearing a purple cape down to her ankles, embroidered with intricate, swirling lines. She was holding a long crystal wand in one hand and a textbook in the other. A youngish but chiseled face made her look slightly strict.

"I came to help you, see how all your injuries are healed? You can call me the Sorceress. And we are sisters in magic. Witches."

Funnily enough, I believed her. I had always felt like I was something *different*. And this was proof of it. Perhaps my pain was proof enough.

"How will you help me?"

"I will be your teacher—practically and *morally*. You will be free of pain, and benevolent, Ezmia. First I'll have to bring you to the Otherworld—the magical plane."

"There are more people with powers?" Relief flooded me. I wasn't the only one.

"Yes, like myself; and like a godmother, I rescue them from *that* inhospitable world. Humans are cruel. Their world is torn apart by war, and yet they have the nerve to be frightened of witches—when they find us, they experiment on us. Finding my sisters isn't easy, but I felt your magic in Hong Kong—and in the end, saw your shield."

She held my hand gently. "But you *will* have to say farewell to your friend."

"Are you okay with that?" I asked Alice, knowing how much she and I needed each other.

She steeled herself and nodded slowly, placing her hand on mine and the Sorceress's. "I'm sad…but proud of you." Her voice finally strengthened, and her eyes shone with hope, for the first time in four bloody years. "But you'll come back to fight for us street children—right?"

I nodded, holding back tears. "I'll fight for *peace*, Alice. Chinese, Japanese—we all need peace. Not revenge."

With that, I got up and embraced her. "Thank you, Alice," I whispered. "We're sisters too."

"Ready to go now?" asked the Sorceress, drawing a white circle in the air with her finger. It expanded like the wings of an angel.

And with that, I stepped into the light, taking the greatest step of my life. Out of the past and into the future. We were orphans no longer.

What the Dreams Whisper

Promise
Trisha Rumjahn

Humans are the superior race on Earth; or so we think. But we've become so twisted and selfish, that our fight for power has destroyed the human race.

But there are some pros apart from the cons, like teleportation and flight.

And one that nobody thought was possible—we could conquer death, become immortal, rise from the dead...

People say that the sky's the limit, but there's always a limit. We can't just have everyone from a thousand years ago come back to life, right?

No, every time one of these actions is performed, somebody else has to die. How could this be worse? Knowing the consequences, it's your choice whether to live forever or not.

August 10, 3022

My attempt to do anything was always interrupted by the constant train of notifications.

There are around a million rules on Earth, but the first and foremost is probably to read every single email you get. And that is a real pain. Because around every two seconds, you'll get an email. And the worst thing is, it might be important, but it usually isn't.

Click. Reminder to read emails. *Click.* Reminder to follow the rules. *Click...* labeled... **Important?**

Stunned, I sat up straight and scrolled downward, scanning the screen.

Olive Bennett,

We are pleased to inform you that you have been doing well in your academics.

"That's it? Just congrats on doing well. Is that really important?" I scoffed, scrolling farther down. There was more.

However, you are to head to the Quad on August 17, 3022, to prepare for your demise in order for another member of your community to continue their life.

We wish you a good day.

I took in the email, incredulous. Demise…as in death? How did that relate to me doing well in my academics?

"What is this?" I screeched, throwing a bright blue cushion on the floor.

In a week. I was condemned to death.

I'd heard of this. Being sacrificed for somebody else's immortality. But I had never thought I would be the one faced with this fate. "Why me?" I roared, realizing that the control I had over myself was slipping away. I was still human after all.

"Ol? You all right?" My mother poked her sharp face into view. "You know screaming so loud is against the rules."

Another rule.

"I don't care about the rules right now!" I yelled, louder if that was even possible. One glance at the horrified look on my mother's face, and I knew I'd said enough.

"Ol—"

"Sorry, Mom. But how is it important to follow the rules when I'm going to die anyway?"

"D-die? What do you mean?"

What the Dreams Whisper

But I think we both know what I meant. Before I knew it, my mother's arms were around me. I could feel her tears falling onto my shirt and the sweat in her dark hair falling into mine.

But they were all hers. I was too angry to cry or sweat a drop. How unjust of *them*. They thought they owned us; they thought they were our superiors, so almighty. They called themselves "the Rulers"—thinking they had the power to control our lives.

"You're only thirteen. If anything I should be sacrificed. This shouldn't be happening to you, honey." My mother wept.

"I told you to drop 'honey,' Mom. And this isn't going to happen to me. I'm not going to let them kill me."

I promised myself I would make that come true. But I only had a week. I've always been a rebel, not having liked the system the Rulers set up. Immersed in the technology as I was like everyone else was, I found a way to hack into their computer systems.

If I was going to let them kill me for somebody else, which I didn't plan on, I had to at least find out who that somebody else was.

And I was back to clicking through emails, pictures, folders, and files. My room suddenly felt so silent. I knew I had limited time—I might be firewalled out of their server at any time.

And then I found it. The file I needed. I scrolled through the pages, finally finding *that one*. At the top of the screen was a picture of me. My name, my dark hair, my dark eyes.

And below my picture was a picture of a boy. That must be the person who signed up for immortality. Suddenly, I couldn't feel my fingers and toes anymore and my muscles seemed to go numb. Why? Because I recognized that sleek brown hair, just slightly draping over his eyes. Those deep blue eyes I looked into every day on the screen. That handsome grin I saw so often.

Hastily, I took a cloddish screenshot, feeling my chest rise up and down, not even bothering to open it up again for another round of dings coming from the red and white mail icon.

I had to call him. I had to ask him.

The *ding* from the computer signaled he was on the other end of the line. "Aidan? D-did you apply for…" So rarely did I stutter.

"Yeah, I did," he replied.

That's what I liked about my best friend. Always so honest. Yes. *My best friend.*

"How could you," I asked bluntly, "knowing that someone would die for you?"

"It wasn't actually me who applied—but that's beside the point. Ol, why are you getting so worked up?"

I looked straight into the camera. "Because I'm the one who'll be killed. I hacked into their systems."

The shock that was displayed on his face was funny enough to make a meme—but I just wasn't in the mood to take a screenshot.

"What? No—that's not—there must be a way to cancel it," he fumbled.

I could hear his fingers moving swiftly across the keyboard, his mouse clicking.

"It won't let me unconfirm it," he said.

I could tell he was struggling to keep his voice sturdy. Another thing I like about my best friend. Always trying to be calm, no matter the situation.

I sighed.

"Hey, it'll be all right," he soothed as I fought hard to swallow.

"I'm all right. I'll do it for you, anyway," I replied, meeting his cool blue eyes.

"No, Ol, we'll find a way—"

"No. Thousands of people go through this, too. Why should I be any different?"

"Because you're my best friend! It's not right," he protested.

"But other people don't know who they're dying for."

"A lot of people know how to hack, Ol. It's the thirtieth century," Aidan pointed out.

True. But I would do it for him in a heartbeat, I realized.

"You can't change my mind," I replied stubbornly, "but be there when it happens, okay? The seventeenth." I was surprised by how collected my voice was.

I could almost feel his gaze burning through the screen, and I thought he was going to argue, but all he said was, "I will," and in a second, his face became a black screen.

August 17, 3022

This was it. Today was the day my life would end and my best friend's would continue forever. I stood in the bustling

Quad, torn between wondering how it would work with the number of people around me and fighting the urge to panic and run.

A hand grabbed mine. The gentle touch was all I needed to know who it was. I didn't even need to look at that brown hair or those blue eyes, but I did because I knew it would be the last time I saw my best friend.

Arms flung around me. "Promise me you won't cry," he whispered in my ear.

"You know I never do," I replied, my voice muffled.

"Just promise."

"I promise."

"Olive Bennett?" a gruff voice sounded.

I turned to a masked man in white who presumably worked for the Rulers.

"That's me," I said, arms crossed, sounding confident and holding back any tears. Just so that I wouldn't break my promise.

The man led us into a little house that I had passed by so many times, but I had never gone inside it. This was my first time—and my last.

"Step there," he ordered, motioning to a circle drawn on the floor. I looked at Aidan, one last time, his face unreadable.

"It won't hurt. By the count of three, you'll just disappear and it'll all be over," the man said.

The words were meant as calming, but he had a slightly menacing tone. To me, just disappearing was so much worse.

Before I could think any more, a cool feminine voice counted, "One…two…three…"

What the Dreams Whisper

I braced myself, reminding myself again not to cry…but I never vanished. No. Instead, I was pushed over so hard onto the stony ground, but my chest was still moving up and down. I could still see the rock walls of the house and the masked man…but I couldn't see Aidan.

Realization hit me hard in the gut—he saved me.

He shoved me—and fell into the circle himself.

The masked man…I could only see his eyes, but I could tell he was flabbergasted. He ran out of the stone house. I was alone.

So I sank to the floor. Tears flowed from my eyes. *I cried.*

So this was what he had planned.

I could almost hear his voice echoing in my ear—

I'm alive, but—

I broke my last promise to him.

A Rare Gift
Liana Chan

This story begins at Efil Academy, a grand and majestic place. Twelve-year-old Anala Moore woke up one morning to the sound of classical music fading in and out. She found herself in the middle of a grand entrance. Large spiral staircases on each side, a harp playing on its own, and the air smelled of freshly cut roses. She wasn't quite sure how she ended up here, but her attention quickly shifted toward a scruffy black-haired boy running toward her with his arms flailing about.

"You're awake! You're awake!" exclaimed the boy.

Anala gave a small smile of relief to see another person, not caring much about his disheveled appearance.

"Sorry if I sound rude, but who are you?" Anala said in the most polite way she could.

"They call me Ash! I'm not sure what my real name is, but when I arrived, I was covered in ashes, so, Ash, it is! What's your n— Oh…sorry, you probably don't have a name yet." He frowned, regretting having asked her.

"My name's Anala. Why would you assume I didn't have a name?" she snapped.

"Oh, sorry, I didn't mean to offend you. Less than a handful of the newcomers remember their names. Anyway hurry!" Ash said, tugging Anala's arm. "We've gotta get to class!"

Before Anala could reply, Ash quickly grabbed her hand and dashed down the hall, making a left turn and then two rights and arriving at Room 1717. They took their seats among several other students who were of similar age.

"Greetings, as most of you know, my name is Ms. Nossel. Today, we will be studying the true forms of kindness," declared a red-headed figure in all black with pale skin.

"Oo, this is going to be good!" Ash whispered to Anala.

Anala stared at Ash, waiting to find some form of a sign he was being sarcastic.

"What kind of class is this? Who learns kindness at school...?" Anala murmured under her breath. Her eyes were getting heavy without realizing it, and she quickly dozed off into a deep slumber. Suddenly, Anala was surrounded by blazing fire crackling all around her. Piercing screams engulfed the smoky air.

"HELP! SOMEBODY HELP!" a familiar voice called in the distance.

Anala's heart beat faster and faster, yet she could not move.

"Anala!" a voice shouted.

She awoke.

She jolted out of her seat, panting. The whole class stared in horror as Ash frantically examined Anala's forehead to feel if she had a fever.

"Anala, are you all right?" Ms. Nossel asked.

As Anala calmed down, she cleared her throat and said, "Sorry, I must have dozed off for a second and just had a bad dream."

At that moment, an ear-splitting gong repeatedly rang throughout the halls. It was time for lunch. As all the other students rushed to the dining hall, Anala dragged her feet.

"What's wrong, Anala? Is everything all right?"

"I'm fine," said Anala. "I just had a bad dream, that's all."

She could see the worry in Ash's face and didn't dare say more in fear of her nightmare scaring him too. He quickly grabbed her hand and ran as fast as his feet could carry him until they arrived in front of two large brass doors. The doors automatically opened to their surprise, and a gush of wind pushed them inside. Anala was stunned by the rows upon rows of old books on the bookshelves. Polished lights hung from the ceiling, and tiny pots of rosemary, tulips, violets, and clovers swayed from side to side, rocking in their hanging planters.

"This is the library," said Ash. "I thought we needed a special knock to enter."

Anala didn't reply.

She was bewitched by the sight of the majestic room with color-tinted skylights and floor-to-ceiling glass shelves that encased thousands of books. Suddenly, the shelves caught aflame and the room faded into blackness.

"HELP SOMEBODY, PLEASE HELP ME!" cried the same familiar voice. She clutched her chest in panic and fainted.

"ANALA!" screamed Ash. "Nurse, help!"

Anala quickly recovered before Ash could scream once more. "Fire! There was a fire!" Anala called out. Ash shot Anala a worried look and scanned the room, looking for any signs of fire around them.

No nurse came but Ash just sitting with her calmed her down. His disheveled appearance yet calm and caring character was quite odd but comforting to Anala. A deep grumbling emanated from

Ash's stomach.

"Oops!" Ash said, slightly blushing from embarrassment.

Anala let out a small giggle and said, "Go have lunch. I'll be fine, I promise. Thanks though, for being so nice to me from the moment I arrived here."

"Are you sure? I'm happy to stay just in case you have one of your nightmares again. My stomach can wait—" An even louder grumble filled the air.

"Go, go. I'll find something to read to get my mind off the nightmares and find you after lunch," Anala insisted.

After Ash left, Anala wandered around the magnificent library, admiring the plethora of books that towered over her. Her gaze stumbled upon a wooden book with no title. Anala laughed, thinking of the concept of a secret book latch and how obvious that would be. She reached out and tugged, not actually expecting to reveal a secret passageway. Nothing happened. She let out a small chuckle at how silly it was to even try and began scanning the other books nearby. Suddenly she heard clanking noises as the bookshelf started shifting by itself. The bookshelf slid to the side and revealed a staircase.

Anala walked down the steps and stopped. There wasn't any dust in the room, meaning someone had regularly visited this secluded place. Anala stopped before a bookshelf and traced her hand over what she realized were files. Hundreds of files lay upon the shelf, neatly arranged.

Azalani Protagia, Ann Cordenni, Azalea Hilda, Ansel Jones, Anala Moore...

She stopped when she saw her own name written on a red binder. Anala grabbed the folder and opened it. She felt her heart drop and was in complete shock. Her lips trembled as she read the page aloud.

Anala Moore engulfed in flames by the fire she started

At 10:00 p.m. on Christmas day, Anala Moore sneaked into the Thomases' house and accidentally dropped an oil lamp that lit the place in flames. The entire Thomas family survived except for their twelve-year-old son, Link, now known as Ash. The girl sadly did not make it, and the reason she snuck into the house was still unknown. However, it was later revealed by the girl's parents that Anala wanted to give Link a stuffed bear as a gift to mend his lonely heart. The girl's mother had tearfully prayed for her daughter and the boy to find peace, thus alarming the angels to have the children taken to Efil Academy for a second chance to experience a friendship of pure love and kindness.

Anala's hands began to tremble. She'd never thought that she was capable of such a thing.

And if what she had read were true, then she'd just killed her new friend. She could hear light footsteps coming toward her.

"Anala?" Ms. Nossel gasped.

Anala fell to her knees and pleaded, "Please tell me, is this true? Is Ash really Link?"

Ms. Nossel paused before saying, "Well, yes. I didn't mean for you to find out this way.

You were given a second chance to be the best and only friend Ash has ever had. Will you tell him the truth? "

Anala nodded and said, "Even though what I did was a horrible accident, he deserves to know the truth. But what is this place? Are we dead?"

Ms. Nossel pursed her lips and said, "Actually, Anala, do you know why it's called Efil Academy? Read it backward. Efil reads as 'Life.' Here at Efil, you have a second chance to go back in time, while in life you should always be either present or looking forward. After Link died,

he arrived here and knew of your kindness. He agreed to stay here to help you gain acceptance of your past and realized you deserve a second chance. Had you both lived, your simple gift to him would have changed his life forever, and the kindness you showed would have lived on and been a beacon of light for him even in the darkest of times till the end. He insisted that you be given a second chance and begged for the opportunity to have a friend just once."

Anala's eyes filled with tears as Ash appeared in the corner of her eye. She called out, "Link! I mean, Ash…I did something horrible."

Ash smiled and said, "The fire? Yeah, I know. I really miss my parents, but they taught me that the meaning of life is to help others, but I never had a friend to help until you. The only thing I really wanted in life…was a friend." Ash began to glow as Anala's heart started to panic.

"What's happening to him?" Anala exclaimed.

Ms. Nossel smiled as Ash reached out his hand.

"Thank you for giving me a chance to finally help someone. But not just anyone, a friend," Ash said as he faded.

As he did, a bright light consumed Anala, and she returned to the Thomases' house, stuffed bear in hand.

It's not often one receives the rare gift of a second chance, but when you do, use it for kindness.

A Blank Page
Cassidy Brown

"I'm sorry, Mrs. Phillips, I just don't know what happened!" Paige insisted, waving her unfinished paper carelessly as she talked. "I really meant to finish it. I even took it home over the weekend, but I just got so caught up in all of my family issues, and couldn't find the time to care about any of the topics you gave us to write about."

"Well, I'm very sorry you felt that way, Paige, but unless I get a letter from a parent or guardian, I can't give you credit," said the teacher.

"But my dad wouldn't write a letter. You know that."

"I know your family situation is tough, but I've made enough exceptions for people to notice. The most I can give you is one more day. Do you think that would be enough time?"

"Of course! Thank you, Mrs. Phillips, I won't disappoint you!" Paige leaned over her teacher's desk to hug her briefly, but then pulled back.

"Are you sure this is all right? The last thing I would want is for you to get in trouble," Paige worried.

"Yes, of course! Just go home and get started so that you have something to turn in tomorrow!" Mrs. Phillips said, shooing her student out the door.

"Right, of course! Goodbye Mrs. Phillips, have a great night!"

"Goodbye, Paige. You too," the teacher called after her as she raced out the door.

As the girl disappeared from view, the teacher's hand dropped, and she leaned back in her chair, removing her glasses to rub her eyes.

***

As Paige waited in the parking lot for her dad to pick her up, she stared at the blank paper that was supposed to hold her description of a past memory.

As the last car left the parking lot, drizzle turned to downpour, and with the realization that her dad wasn't coming, the young girl was left to hold the drenched paper over her head as she raced home, blinded by the pouring rain.

By the time she reached her front door, the rain had calmed, and she walked inside.

Her dad was sitting on their worn-out sofa, staring at the television, but she could tell he wasn't watching.

"You forgot again," Paige said.

Her dad turned to her, but his gaze wandered back to the screen without a response.

She raced up to her room and took a fresh piece of paper out of her desk drawer.

Thump thump thump, Paige's pencil drummed against her desk. As her eyes found her old family photo, she found herself filled with inspiration, and she leaned forward, pencil moving swiftly across the page.

My Story
by Paige Peterson

"So they went off together. But wherever they go, and whatever happens to them on the way, in that enchanted place on the top of the

Forest, a little boy and his Bear will always be playing," Mom finished the book with a sigh.

I was so quiet, you could hear the soft thud as the cover met the pages, and Christopher Robin and his favorite bear faded away. I wondered where they went because I just knew that they weren't gone.

So I asked my mom, "Where did they go?"

She laughed and pulled me in for a hug. "They are always there, even if we can't see them. There are some stories that don't end once the words are gone because they are too real to be made up."

"Then why doesn't the story go on forever?"

"Because all the things it makes you feel are too real, and when something is real, it has the ability to last as long as the earth goes on."

I cuddled closer. "I think that's true."

Just then, I heard the front door slam shut.

"Daddy!" I called as he entered the room. I smiled up at him as he took off his coat with a sigh and sat down on the bed next to me.

"Tough day at work?" Mom asked.

He nodded and stretched out next to us.

I cuddled close to both of them, immersed in my bubble of happiness. That's when I realized something.

"Hey! We're like a grilled cheese sandwich!"

Mom and Dad looked at each other and then down at me before bursting with laughter. And before I knew it, I was laughing too.

Suddenly, Paige's pencil slipped from her hand, but instead of reaching to grab it, her hands flew to her ears, trying to block the sound of her family's laughter echoing in her brain. She cried out, but it was no use. She felt as though she was being attacked, her own mind her competitor, her memory its weapon. And what was she left with? What could she use to fight back?

She lay on the floor, tears streaming down her face and turning into a wet puddle on the sand-colored wood. She imagined she was Alice from the tales told to her by her mother when she was young. Tales of a girl that went down a rabbit hole, nearly drowned in a puddle of her giant tears, and still made it out alive.

If only I was as brave as Alice, she thought. *Then I might be able to win.*

She kept thinking about that, until she heard a voice in the back of her head.

"You can win, you know," the voice said.

"But how?" Paige responded.

"You just have to put in enough effort to change the tides."

***

Downstairs, Paige found her dad where he had been when she got home, still watching the same show.

"Dad," she called. "Can I talk to you?"

"Sure," her dad responded without turning from the TV. "What is it?"

"Can you please turn off the television?" Paige responded.

He pressed the remote, and with a soft click, the screen went black.

"Dad, I miss you. I miss the family we used to be. Even though only Mom died that night, it feels like I lost both of you."

Her dad looked taken aback, but his face softened into an understanding yet sad expression.

"I'm sorry. I really am. And I knew you felt this way. I hate that you feel this way still. But it's hard. It's really very hard for me because even though my body's here with you, my mind is up there with her. You know this, and I believe that some part of you will always be with her, no matter how hard you try to push past it. But I do try for you. I don't want to make you miserable," Paige's dad said, breathing deeply, as though he had been holding in his breath nearly as long as his own thoughts.

"I know, Dad. Can we both work to change, even if it's just saying hello in the morning and goodbye at night?"

Her dad looked up at her and smiled.

"I can promise that," he said, holding out his hand.

Paige shook his hand with a laugh. And he laughed too. And the girl knew that somewhere out there, her mom was laughing with them.

Zoo Misfits

Sarah Swan

Gerrie hated his nickname. After all, who could put up with being called Mr. Short Neck all the time. Why did everyone have to be so mean? Gerrie was normal in every way except his height. His neck was only a foot long. Because of this, he was teased and disliked among the other giraffes. Gerrie's parents were ashamed, and they pretended that they didn't see the shoves or hear the hurtful words.

In the huge safari pen of the North Carolina Zoo, there were places to hide from the other animals. One of these hideouts was an old acacia tree. For long hours Gerrie would sit under its shade, out of sight from the other giraffes. The tree was so old that its bark was peeling off like a snake shedding its skin. Its bare limbs stretched out over a large grassy plain, which was now tan like the dead leaves of the fall trees. It was a great tree to hang out under, and best of all, it wasn't near the lion's pen. The cats shared a boundary on the far side of the habitat. They somehow knew when a giraffe was near and scared every animal around by growling and snarling at anyone that came near. Except of course, the humans. The lions just slept around them.

One day Gerrie was dozing under the acacia when he heard a noise from behind the tree that startled him. He went around its massive trunk and gasped. Lying there, stirring from sleep, was a zebra. It was an all-white zebra with not a speck of black or brown on it. Even on his nose there was no color. Now awake, it was the zebra's turn to gasp. "You're so short," he said.

Gerrie frowned. Even though he couldn't change it, Gerrie HATED his height. People always stared and whispered behind his back. "And you're, um, really white," Gerrie answered.

The zebra looked down. "I get told that a lot."

"I get told I'm short a lot," Gerrie said. "What's your name anyway?"

"My name's Zeb," the zebra said, starting to smile.

They were, for a few moments, unsure of what else to say. Gerrie broke the silence. "How old are you, Zeb?"

"I'm six full-moons old," Zeb answered.

"I am seven full-moons old," Gerrie replied. "Say, how about we be friends?"

"Okay," Zeb said, "but only on one condition."

"What's that?" Gerrie asked while cocking his head to the right.

"We don't tease each other."

They both laughed. For the rest of the day, Gerrie and Zeb played, swapped jokes, and just hung out. But soon the wonderful day was over, and they said their goodbyes and left, but not before planning a meeting for the following day.

Zeb and Gerrie continued to grow their friendship around the acacia tree. Their favorite things to do were playing tag, playing hide-and-go-seek tag, and having races. They both loved to run.

One freezing day, the sky filled with clouds, and it began to snow. And snow it did! The storm soon turned into a blizzard. All the animals ran as fast as they could into a smelly building at the corner of the pen. No one was calm, but a certain young mother giraffe was very restless. She was going around the room like she was searching for someone. "My calf is gone," she suddenly cried out. "The storm came, and in the confusion, she must have been lost."

The leaders of the giraffe and zebra packs started forming search parties. Of course, neither Gerrie nor Zeb were picked to go, so they just went together to help. Just then there was an elephant-size crash from over by the lion's den where a massive tree had fallen. It was a giant oak, laden heavy with snow. When it fell, it created a wooden bridge that connected the two pens.

"Zeb, where'd you go?" Gerrie yelled into the snow.

"Look, I'm right here beside you."

"Oh," Gerrie said. "It's hard to see you because of your white fur. You look invisible." They kept walking. The snow seemed to slow now, for they were under a tree. "It might take a while to find this calf," Gerrie said. "After all, there's a lot of space to cover, and this storm is pretty bad, don't you think?"

Zeb didn't answer. Gerrie looked at him and saw that he was staring at something in the distance, trembling. Gerrie followed Zeb's gaze, and barely stifled a cry. About ten feet in front of them was a lion—in their pen—stalking the baby giraffe.

"What do we do?" whispered Zeb.

"We've got to save her," Gerrie whispered back. "Zeb, Go get help, I'll try to distract him."

"But it'll be too late," Zeb whispered back in a high-pitched voice. "We have to do something now. I've got a plan. No time to explain. Go distract him."

Gerrie confused the lion by acting like he was the baby giraffe. It was a good thing he was so small, or the lion would have known he was an imposter. As Gerrie did all of this, he watched for Zeb. He barely saw the camouflaged albino zebra approaching the lion from behind. Gerrie tensed. *What is Zeb up to? I hope he knows what he's doing.* "Run, little one," Gerrie yelled to the baby giraffe, who was frozen with terror.

When the baby sprinted away, Zeb made his move from behind. He charged the lion. With an angry snort, he jumped high in the air. The lion turned his way just in time to get a face full of two colorless hooves.

The baby giraffe was long gone, running to hide in the trees behind them. Then for the first time Gerrie and Zeb saw their audience. All the animals from the pen, including both of their parents and the mother of the baby giraffe were watching. The lion lay still as death on the fresh snow.

Zeb and Gerrie were accepted by the others that day. For as long as the two misfits lived at the zoo, they were never teased about their height or color again.

"For the Lord does not see as man sees; for man looks at the outward appearance, but the Lord looks at the heart." —1 Samuel 16:7

What the Dreams Whisper

Conundrum
Brishti Adhikari

The sound of leaves crunching echoed through the trees. Your back was propped up against one of them. You knew something was coming. As the footsteps stopped, your moment of relief was over with the sound of an ear-piercing scream.

. . .

Vee woke up to the sound of Uno cards falling on the floor. He grabbed his glasses off his nightstand, glancing at the time. 2:02 in the morning.

"Not fair! Why do you always win? I bet you're cheating," muttered a girl with flaming pink hair. This was Arwen, one of Vee's best friends. "Let's play again!"

"That was our thirteenth round, Arwen," said an amber-eyed boy with light brown hair, making eye contact with Vee with an exasperated sigh. Meet Oakley, Vee's best friend for life.

"Whatever. Ooo, what if we go to the FOREST. The spooky one outside Vee's—" Arwen glanced at the bed, expecting to see a sleeping Vee. "Oh, you're awake! I was gonna suggest we pour ice on your head again."

"Please don't," Vee said, shuddering at the memory. Arwen had gotten two pounds of ice and dumped it on his head so he'd play Chutes and Ladders with them. "I'll go to the creepy forest if you don't pour ice on my head."

"As long as you don't chicken out. Knowing you, I'm going to have to pour *four* pounds of ice on you this time."

"Woah," Oakley interrupted. "We are *not* going to that weird forest, especially with that killer dude lurking around here."

Arwen rolled her eyes. "This is a democracy, not a dictatorship."

"Isn't it more of an oligarchy?"

"We're not wealthy old men."

"Anyway," Vee cut in, "forest time. Should we bring anything?"

"What about matches?" Arwen suggested. "It's bound to be cold." It was mid October, which was the point where it was too cold for hot weather, but too hot for snow.

"No," Vee said immediately. "Nothing fire related. Except for a fire extinguisher, if anyone brought one of those for some weird reason. What if you set your hand on fire, Arwen?"

"It was one time," she hissed. "Technically it wasn't even my fault," she added as she picked up the Uno cards. "The matches have a mind of their own."

Oakley rolled his eyes, swinging a small bag over his shoulder. "C'mon, let's go. I'd rather not hear this stupid story again, even if it means we have to go to the creepy forest."

Arwen grinned. She grabbed her Converse and started running out of Vee's bedroom. You could hear her footsteps rush down the stairs.

"Don't be too loud! You're going to wake up my sister," Vee whisper-yelled.

Oakley sighed. "She's going to get lost. Let's catch up to her." He exited the room without another word, leaving Vee to himself.

Vee had a feeling that this was a bad idea. He took another glance at the clock, which now read 2:23. The last time they'd been to the forest at this time, they were seven. That time, it had been Vee's idea.

They had just moved to their current house, and he was intrigued by the forest. Back then, the leaves on the trees were a vibrant green in the spring and stunning orange in the autumn. Even in the harsh winter, the forest still managed to look beautiful with all the deadness. The snow had no yellow spots, and it instead covered all the trees in a pristine manner.

Arwen wasn't as pumped to explore the forest the first time around. She insisted it'd be boring, as it looked too perfect. Oakley then convinced her that nothing was perfect, and there was a hidden mystery behind it all. Arwen was down.

Over time, the forest deteriorated with pollution and fires of sorts, giving it a creepy atmosphere. It had been a hot minute since they'd been there. It seemed to be off.

"I have an idea. Let's play hide-and-seek."

That one sentence ruined it all.

***

"Twenty-eight, twenty-nine, thirty," Oakley yelled into the abundance of trees. He kicked the dirt as he began to run through the woods. The wind blew vigorously. Oakley quickly zipped his jacket tighter. It had been a bad idea to go to the forest in pajamas.

After a few minutes of looking behind trees, Oakley gave up. This was going to take ages and they were probably going to get in huge trouble. Once he found his friends, he was going to drag them back to Vee's house. Except, he couldn't find them.

Oakley looked underneath beds of clovers to see if Arwen had magically shrunk herself. Oakley didn't find Arwen, but he found a four-leaf clover.

He left it, but he shouldn't have.

It was hard to see in the dark. They wouldn't realize if Oakley just left, right? He looked at the trees surrounding him, then began to weave through them.

The sound of boots crunching leaves intensified as Oakley ventured through the woods. It was only his boots making that noise.

A *swish* pierced the air, causing Oakley to turn around.

An arrow had stabbed a tree, barely missing him by luck.

Suddenly, a tall man with slicked back hair appeared from one of the clusters of trees. He looked like he worked in an office cubicle, with tired eyes and a suit. Who wears a suit at two in the morning? Why was he in Stoa Forest?

"There's more of those," said the ominous man.

"What?" Oakley diverted his eyes to where the man was looking. The arrow in the tree. Oh *no*. He didn't have Arwen's impulsivity. He couldn't improvise with a branch!

The man stepped closer. "I've seen your little friends here too," he said, like he was reading Oakley's mind. "I'll make a deal with you."

"Choose carefully."

***

Arwen's hiding spot was in a tree. She'd always loved climbing them. It was one of her go-to hiding spots, but

What the Dreams Whisper

Oakley never managed to find her. She was in a tree that was in a secluded area of the forest. She was surprised to see Oakley looking up at the trees.

There was something shiny in his pocket.

Something told Arwen to climb down.

She slowly stepped on the branch below her, then swung onto the ground.

"Uh, found you?" Oakley said with confusion in his voice.

"I was about to fall," Arwen lied.

Arwen and Oakley had never really gotten along perfectly. Vee had introduced them, but they just didn't click. It wasn't awkward between them, but they didn't have much in common besides Vee. They would do things that friends did like play Uno at one in the morning, but nothing was there.

Arwen didn't think Oakley'd go this far.

"So, you're going to hate me for this, but…" Oakley trailed off.

Arwen rolled her eyes. "Spit it out."

"I think I need to show you instead." The nervousness in his voice had changed to certainty instead. Maybe Arwen was hearing things.

"Go ahead."

Oakley took the shiny thing that Arwen had been eyeing earlier out of his pocket. Her eyes widened.

***

Vee's back rested against the bark of the tree he was hiding behind. He was close to falling asleep, with the breeze brushing against his neck.

Just as Vee closed his eyes, they were forced back open by a scream.

It sounded like the one he heard when Arwen saw a spider. Or the one when she bleached her hair and it ended up falling out because she didn't want to get it done professionally. Except this scream was more painful to listen to.

It was quiet again, but the silence was now loud.

Vee's heart felt like it was going to jump out of his chest. He stood up and slowly made his way to where the scream came from. Scenarios flooded his mind.

"Well, I have no use for you now," said a voice.

Vee hid behind the nearest tree, his breathing heavy.

"What do you mean? You said you'd keep your end of the deal," said a familiar voice.

Oakley.

Oh no. What had he gotten them into?

Vee put together the pieces.

"No!"

Oakley screamed. The same scream as Arwen.

Vee was silent. He stood behind the tree until he heard leaves being crunched on the ground. This wasn't supposed to happen.

Vee slowly made his way to where he thought Oakley was, and he regretted it. A silver arrow pierced his neck. His face was lifeless. Vee wanted to puke. He leaned over Oakley's body.

"I knew there was another one."

Vee jolted upward. It was a man dressed in a suit. There was a red spot on his white tie.

Vee ran. He ran as fast as he could, dodging the trees as he did. He wasn't losing himself to the man in the suit. He was

What the Dreams Whisper

too young to go anyway. But apparently not Arwen and Oakley.

Was Arwen even gone?

That question was answered once Vee found her body.

Her pink hair was stained red at the ends. Her glasses were shattered, and the bracelets that were on her wrist had mostly been broken. Except for one. It was blue and white with a star charm. Vee picked it up and slid it onto his own wrist. He was just about to leave, until he realized Arwen's jacket pocket was unzipped and empty.

She kept matches there. She always did, even when Vee asked her not to.

The smell of smoke began to form.

Vee began to run again. He just needed to get out. Red and orange began to form in the corners of his eyes. It got warmer and warmer until he was surrounded.

He could see the exit, just a few more moments—

He tripped.

Big Heart
Alex Jiang

A Tokyo day dawned crisp and clear. The sun poured through Mark Murata's window. Scrolling on his tablet with his long white fingers, Mark sipped his black morning coffee and ate buttered toast. Sure enough, his perfect peace was interrupted. A message, ringing in his half-machine brain, informed him that there was a problem at Big Heart. He merely nodded to close it.

He suppressed a moan and returned to work for a premature shift. He got into his Mini Cooper, which was growling like it was sick, and drove to work, awash in the city's ever-brighter lights. With his still-tired mind, he only suspected that someone had become trapped in an elevator or something.

***

Mark was a regular employee at Big Heart, a Japanese corporation. It was 2032, and Big Heart was one of the largest companies in the world, with the goal of implanting microchips into humans and developing devices to help human bodies avoid brain tumors, heart attacks, and a growing number of other diseases.

When he arrived at Big Heart, it was chaos. Stacks of papers were dropped into grids and towers everywhere, shedding their feathery loads as black suits swarmed around them. It was like a swarm of racoons being discovered in a trash can and scattering everything everywhere.

Behind him, Mark heard someone say, "Sir, sir!"

It was Larry Lim. Security team deputy—to Mark. He ran up to him as fast as he could, pushing people aside with his augmented arm as they tried to scatter.

Panting, he said, "Sir, you have a major problem! Someone has infiltrated Big Heart's firewall! The hacker has disabled all our microchips, in human bodies and devices! People are dying all over the place, and hospitals are in crisis right now."

Mark was shaken when he heard this, as if he'd opened the door on an Arctic storm. He dashed to the HQ server room, shoving aside its scratched, warped metal maintenance door.

It was too late. Everyone in the room was dead. Over thirty people were thrown to the ground, their hearts ripped out, and some of their body parts severed from their bodies. Everyone was in a state of disbelief. Some cried, some screamed; others jabbered about the scene, eyes wide and glassy. Mark zoned out in his uneasiness, but then—

A man. A black hoodie and long black cargo pants tucked into boots. Standing in a corner behind the shivering crowd. No ID. In the darkness, Mark saw metal gleaming behind his back—a blade.

With his chest pounding, Mark pulled out his handgun and charged at the figure like a bull. But as he came within a blade's distance, the man dissolved into a digital cloud.

A cloaking device.

Now this was a real professional. You felt it in your bones. The terrified techies in the room had run out screaming. Mark followed them, yelling the alert into his radio.

As he ran into the office's common room, a live video was playing on the jumbo TV. Everyone stared.

The ransom note video stated that the company Big Heart had to pay four billion dollars to stop the virus. This was not unheard of in itself, but few hackers can boast this of their virus:

I will tear apart 70 percent of Big Heart users if the trade is not completed within seven hours.

Then the video ended.

Everyone was stunned and began to panic, spreading rumors and debating what to do. Then, at a slow pace, a black shadowy figure entered the large room. Everyone fell silent when they heard the CEO's voice.

The CEO merely stated, "Activate the ransom protocol. Ask for backup."

Then he vanished into thin air.

Standard security protocol, thought Mark. *Activate cloaking device, get to your office, lesser employees need not see you or know much.*

The chitchat of course resumed.

Everyone below-clearance is wondering what "backup" stands for.

***

The CEO was sitting in his office, surrounded by various animal skins, including a tiger's skin for the floor, and four different types of bear heads on the wall. Hunting was an expensive habit indeed in the 2030s.

The detective swept through the door of the CEO's office with three large men. A six-foot-tall man with a silver arm entered the room. His face was hooded by his cloakable raincoat, but it was clear that both his eyes were augmented. One of his legs was silver as well. Some people couldn't shake off affection for at least one of their flesh limbs, after all. He was carrying a large backpack full of belongings and smoking a cigarette at the same time, clamping it firmly as his jaw was set in anger. The other two

What the Dreams Whisper

men were dressed simply in black suits, but their eyes were so heavily augmented they preferred to hide them behind sunglasses indoors. These guys meant business.

The bag spat out two different types of pills for the two men in black suits. Swallowing them without hesitation, they stood poised, limbs a little spread out, knowing what was coming next.

It was a surreal sight. Their bodies mutated. Their arms became so big that they could have shattered the reinforced ceiling and brought the room above crashing down. Their height also increased, albeit slowly, to eight feet.

They stood, flexed their arms a little, and took off their sunglasses, revealing cold metal eyes. They were ready for action.

The detective finally spoke:

"We will locate and kill the hacker. Our drones are sweeping the city. It's only a matter of time."

With their cloaking devices, they vanished into thin air.

The CEO was a biotech businessman. But even he would always feel a little unsettled by military-grade cell acceleration.

***

Within minutes, the hacker had tracked the rough location of the ransomware attack. This assault felt straightforward to plan.

They used their cloaking device to position themselves outside the house. It was a large, stately townhouse, its face white and impassive.

The detective took out his C4 charges and blew up the door—

And they entered with the speed of light. Just to see hundreds and hundreds of cyborgs filling the entrance hall, from mosquito drones to giant walkers, waiting for them. It was a trap. The hacker sat in his seat, fingers a cloud over his keyboards, and when he heard the door open, he only said, "Kill them."

The first cyborg's eyes turned as red as the sun, and he began to attack in all directions. The two men charged through like bulls, destroying the cyborg before they could fire their weapons. So the detective took two miniguns from his hands and began shooting so heavily that it looked like falling stars covered the entire sky, peering in its pink impassiveness from a skylight. As cyborgs were being shot left and right, the other two men began punching their way through them and ripping them apart like paper.

One of the detective's bullets struck the hacker, shredding his chest and sending blood and synthetic cyberbrain fluid flying out. As the cyborgs set out to help their creator, it was an ideal opportunity for the two men to run over all of them. When the men were charging the cyborgs, it was too late. The cyborgs self-destructed, not only bringing down the two men but also their own creator. The operation was over.

But the virus did not stop. It had metastasized globally.

The detective's instinct kicked in. Only minutes remained. Panting, he was even slower. There were only two minutes left when the detective returned. When he attempted to enter the server room in the belly of the beast, the blast door was locked, and none other than Lim, conducting a fake evidence-gathering operation, was standing behind it—destroying drives. *He* was the inside man.

The detective roared. *"Out of the way! Open up now!"*

Lim, his jaw set in anger, clammed up and blocked the door. A detective finally kicked it open, throwing Lim to the ground, his metal arm clanging on the floor—

One of the giants jumped on him, enraged, crushing his chest beneath a metal foot.

Thirty seconds left.

The detective slid his data drive into the hostile computer. It clicked like a loaded gun, and the machine gave one last sigh.

Adults, elders, and even children in the crowd outside the building roiled and roared. They clutched at their augmented chests, wailing and gnashing their teeth. Their minds could no longer function in their individual and group breakdown. Soon they curled up and lay, like burned petals.

Outside, blood fell from the sky—from body parts flying from the explosion in the building—as the server room exploded. Lim's body, metal and flesh, was torn apart with his comrades—human and otherwise. The sky, already red from city lights and blotting out the stars for decades, now filled with black smoke, blending the man-made horizon with the filthy streets.

Lim died, but it came at the price of the world's beating metal heart—its Faustian bargain with science.

A Bloody Inheritance
Kristy Chan

The granite-and-marble faces on either side of Manhattan's Fifth Avenue loomed over the crowds below that scurried home at the end of the winter day.

One black car pulled up outside an apartment building, and a middle-aged man in a wheelchair, his broken body curled up and wrapped in cashmere and corduroy, was led out by his valet to its welcoming golden maw.

Soon, his body would be found in a pool of blood in his apartment's office. He'd bought it after selling his family's ancestral home. He thought he could escape the bad memories that had built up, like dark pools, in its shadows. But the emptiness and money of New York would be the death of him. And all that flashed before his eyes before he died was this story.

***

The Mediterranean sea stretched out behind me like wings. Up the hill ahead of me stretched Oia, Santorini—a coral-reef village of white stone cubes. A windmill waved gently at me from above the skyline. I'd spent the day with Penelope, and now we wanted some peace and quiet. I nudged her up a discreet little cobblestoned alley. At its end, the sky loomed, pink and inviting.

A black van pulled up, blocking the sky and casting a shadow over us both.

Before we had time to react, I felt a great, bearlike pair of hands grab me by the shoulder and neck, shoving me forward.

Penelope let out a strangled scream before she was dismissively thrown behind us by my captor, and I felt my chest heaving with pain as I was thrown into the van.

***

Within hours, the news was out. Penelope called the police, and my kidnappers had announced their demands. I'd been taken to a village on the mainland. Sat down on a bare wooden chair by my new friends, I watched the evening news buzz with my name. Adam Bailey IV. I had yet to see or hear from my parents, but I knew the lawyers had been called.

At least I hadn't had my rib broken. I sipped a little cool water and wondered if the thugs would let me open the window.

***

The kidnappers' leader Nicos came into the room. In his gravelly voice, he reported, "You're lucky, boy. Your family is reasonable."

There was a beat.

Nicos practically whispered, "However, we've decided to ask for a greater ransom."

I drew up my chest and looked squarely into his eaglelike brown eyes. "Stick to your agreement. You're already getting a lot out of this," I said.

He can't get greedy. Not now.

His leathery brown face smiled gently—almost sadly. "Your family has everything. That means everything to lose. You're the heir. Let's not underprice you." He turned to the door, his black long coat swaying gently in the breeze.

In one last attempt to salvage the progress made, I shouted, voice quavering. "Wait! I'll give you a way to get my mother to agree to a larger amount."

Uncurling like a praying mantis, I jumped up and punched him with a long hook, straight in the jaw. He reeled backward, his face disfigured by fury. But I failed to dislodge him from the door. He roared for help.

Two gang members charged into the room, shoving me back as I tried to escape. They clamped my head down, left side, onto the table. I struggled to hear voices above me.

"Incentivize…"

Paralyzed with fear, I smelled wood and saw my panting kicking up dust from the table, scattering it in the hot air.

An enforcer returned with a knife. He handed it to Nicos—now grinning from ear to ear.

I felt cold steel begin to slice off my own right ear.

***

"The exchange is happening. They agreed to a fat increase," I heard one of the mafiosi mutter to Nicos outside the door to my humble domain.

"Good. Get the boy."

I heard the clicking of the lock and then the turning of the handle. He stomped inside the room, his face obscured by a black mask. "It's time to go," he said hoarsely.

He pulled me up from my chair and bound my hands in front of me. He put a gag in my mouth but left my eyes uncovered.

The right side of my face was bandaged. The gang had fed me painkillers and ouzo, caring little for the health risks involved; anything to silence my screams. Now I only shivered. News of my ear's delivery to the police had finally been reported.

I was led out into the courtyard of the farmhouse as the sun set. The house was on the edge of an olive grove, just beginning to cast its lengthening shadows over us all. Armed men stood silently around, scanning their environment. It was like a tableau, devoid of life, but alive with tension.

A fat Mercedes, like a black queen bee, hummed along the dirt road to the farm, flanked by a police car. Just like they asked—only one. I felt relieved for a moment. I didn't want a fight breaking out. I saw the cops step out of the car and open the door to my mother Amélie's Merc. She stepped out, my sick and elderly father in his wheelchair behind her. She looked around, her big, beautiful brown eyes scanning the courtyard, desperately looking for me. The moment her eyes latched onto mine, I could see the tension coiled up in her drain away.

We stood on opposite sides in the courtyard. Me with four thugs beside me, armed with revolvers. My mother was with my lawyer, Mr. Lincoln, my father, now hunched over his cane, and three policemen—one plainclothed. Like my new friends, my eyes were naturally drawn to a suitcase carried by Lincoln.

Nicos spoke up first. "Hand over the money and the boy will slowly walk over."

But neither I nor the thugs expected my mother's cool nerves. "You've already injured him, and you've already broken one deal. Time to give us something. We'll throw you the suitcase while I check his injuries here."

The thugs exchanged glances. But sunlight was getting short. Nobody wanted a fight.

Nicos coolly ordered me over with one of his lieutenants, Belen. I felt his fat fist push me gently forward across the courtyard. My heart pounded.

My mother embraced me as soon as I arrived. Turning around, I saw Belen, looking bulky in a flight jacket, nod at Lincoln.

Lincoln threw the suitcase onto the dusty clearing in the middle of the courtyard instead. Belen furrowed his brow in annoyance and briskly marched toward it. Nicos swayed his body a little, instinctively adopting a fighting stance.

While he walked to the suitcase and picked it up, I was led to the Merc. I saw my bandaged head and dried blood in its tinted window.

When I looked back, Belen was one step away from opening the case, and I noticed a flash from somewhere in the forest. I turned back around, now merely steps away from the Mercedes.

Just as I was about to take that final step, that final step into safety, I heard a crack. A gunshot.

Eyes forward, I yanked the car door open, but it was too late. The thugs immediately called for backup, more mafiosi streamed out of the house, sawn-offs and handguns drawn—

But the police were ready too. From the forest, faceless black shadows emerged like ghouls, coalescing in the dying sunlight—a SWAT team, guns roaring.

Belen's hands were already on the case. But as he clicked it open, he gave an animalistic cry. He threw the case at his boss, and it fell open midair.

Some cash tumbled out—and a phonebook. *The Baileys tried to cheat.*

Belen's square head was perforated by a bullet and he fell.

Enraged, Nicos fired his revolver in my direction. I froze in terror. I couldn't move. My mother pushed in front of me, screaming.

A bullet hit my mother's chest. She crumpled to the ground.

"Mother!" I cried, struggling with my rage. I reached out, but a cop shoved me into the car with my father instead.

The Merc roared ahead. Gunshots died out behind me. Flat against its bulletproof glass, contorted by a silent scream, I saw Nicos, with his case, cash, and cronies, disappear into the forest. Mafiosi and SWAT men littered the bloody dirt.

But it was my mother's body, lying in a pool of dark red blood, that would haunt my nightmares forever.

***

As I dictate this letter, I'm looking out my office window at the cold faces of Manhattan's towers. They feel like judges. Maybe I'll face a real judge soon.

I, Adam Bailey IV, was the cause of my kidnapping. I made a deal with the mafia to get myself kidnapped. I ensured Penelope witnessed it.

All I wanted was my family's money. They'd cut me off. It wasn't fair; I'm the eldest son, I'd been prepared to take over the company, and my father was too old to run it. He was clinging to it and making mistakes. If they'd just been willing to overlook a few of my little mistakes, I know I would've done a good job, and my life was meaningless without it. Don't judge me.

For years, I've been torn to pieces over my mother, and now I'm lying here, strapped flat to a wheelchair like I'm about to be toe-tagged already. I'm sorry about what I put my family through, and myself through.

And if you're angry I got the money from my family—with both my parents gone—don't be. Money doesn't help a walking corpse.

It's over now. I'm going to put down my pen and end my life.

What the Dreams Whisper

In the Depths of the Peaceful Forest

Ketki Khadilkar

I stalked through the forests, following the smell. I had caught the scent of a big, plump pig. If I listened really closely and went a bit faster, I could faintly hear its footsteps tromping through the crunchy leaves, which I avoided.

If I haven't told you already, I *love* the sweet, juicy taste of fat, healthy pigs. I will never get tired of pigs. However, pigs are smart and are difficult to hunt and kill.

Coming back to reality, Big Pig (as I had nicknamed my victim) and I were reaching a small clearing. It was the shape of a crooked circle, and sitting in the center was a mud puddle. Big Pig walked to the exact middle of the clearing and sat down to rest. He let out a deep sigh. I decided since he was off-guard, it was time to pounce.

I jumped through the air, hurling myself toward Big Pig. He was looking to the side. Still, he saw me and ducked out of the way. He lunged at me and bared his yellow teeth. *Stupid wolf,* I could practically see him thinking. I dodged his blow and sprinted.

Because I was skinny, I could slide through cracks between trees. Behind me, Big Pig crashed right through them, bruising himself in the process. Rabbits sprang aside. I ran as hard as I could manage. Sweat streamed off my weathered gray fur.

Finally, I came upon a rock cave with a narrow entrance. I squeezed through the coarse crevice, scraping my skin, and stumbled into the dark room. Big Pig glanced in at me and snorted curtly. Then he trotted off. I was safe for now. However, I decided I needed to come up with a clever plan.

I woke up early, and my stomach roared thunderously. Then I remembered what had happened the day before, and the idea I had. My plan would start shortly.

But first, I had to get a snack. I wedged myself through the opening of the small cavern. Right away, I sniffed the fresh odor of a rabbit and spotted its footprints on the ground. It had rained overnight, so there was a blanket of sticky mud carpeting the leafy surface of the earth. I trailed the footprints and soon had the rabbit in view. The rabbit bounded off toward a bush. I hid behind a nearby tree. Then it beckoned its babies to come out of underneath the bush.

This will be a grand breakfast, I thought, drool collecting in a small puddle at my feet.

When the rabbit turned its back to me, I dived at it, killing both the mommy and the two babies. I happily tore through the flesh, leaving nothing besides the bones. Then I got ready to confront Big Pig.

As I got to the clearing, Big Pig was soaking in the mud puddle. I went over my plan a second time, to make sure there weren't any mistakes. Then came the strenuous part, the dreadful part of my plan. I had to wait for a distraction.

Seconds turned into minutes. Minutes turned into hours. Hours turned into endless days. It felt like years before I got lucky.

After a few hours, I heard a sound. *Beep. Beep.* Big Pig spun to face where it was coming from. This was my chance.

I leaped and soared through the air. The birds flew elsewhere in a chatter. The trees above split, and for a second, the sun shone on my body, lighting it up. Big Pig looked up, but it was too late. I crashed down upon him, my claws tearing his muscles apart.

When I was about to take my first bite of victory, I realized the beeping sound had grown louder. *Beep! Beep!* I glanced up to see what it was.

A gigantic machine, as tall as two grown sunflowers stacked on top of each other, was rambling toward me. It started chopping trees down with a saw as big as the tree itself! I turned and ran for my life.

The machine was unexpectedly fast, and it soon caught up to me. *BEEP! BEEP!* I twisted around and tried climbing it, and slipped clear off. I got up and clung to a thick tree for dear life.

Big mistake. The machine chopped the tree down, and me in half. I almost instantly fell off, and then my body crumpled. I stopped moving.

If you come to the forest, you may see both skinny halves of my body coated in blood. The trees are all stumps as far as the eye can see. Nearby is a huge pig lying several feet to one side, his body ripped apart and abandoned. He is lying in a mud puddle. You may come across a few bird nests lying forgotten on the rough dirt. Yet no machines are in sight, nor are there any live animals.

You will never know what really happened in the depths of the peaceful forest.

Countdown
Ishaani Molugu

Lauren Meek rushed down the hallway of Horizon Intermediate, with Josey's hand in hers. She wasn't any normal kid. She was the troublemaking, adventure-seeking, enough-detention-slips-to-wallpaper-her-whole-apartment kind of kid. She raced past and eventually into the old, unused computer lab, aka, Lauren's hang-out room. She clutched a chair to maintain her balance and cowered over her precious treasure. It was more than a treasure; it was a miracle. This is how it came to end up in her scraggly palms:

It all started when she got sent to the principal's office for vandalizing. Of course, she had much better things to do than that. She skipped out the double doors to the left of the cafeteria, into the gymnasium. *Nothing good in here*, thought Lauren, but she still wanted to explore deeper inside because she was bored and had nothing to do. Lauren went farther into the gymnasium and into the gym teacher's office, where she dug out new sports manuals and began reading. Until she heard footsteps.

"Yes, that should be good," the anonymous person said as they walked closer to the gym office.

Lauren dove under the gym teacher's desk and waited. Lauren saw sneakers. And heard a *THUD*.

"Where are the manuals? I put them right here on my desk."

Lauren gasped and looked down at her hands where she held the manuals the gym teacher was looking for. She squirmed back as far as she could to get out of the teacher's sight until she was in the absolute corner. She squished her face against the wall and tried to shrink when something caught her eye. There was a crack in the wall, barely noticeable, with something shimmering inside. She ran over it with her hand and felt a weak spot and stuck her finger in and tugged. The wall came away as if it were paper. She stuck her hand in and felt around. *Just some sort of hole in the wall,* thought Lauren. But as she felt around some more, her hand touched something cold and metal, about the size of her palm. She tried to tug her hand out, but it was stuck.

Five minutes passed and Lauren's arm was starting to cramp when she heard the voices again.

"Leave the manuals, Mrs. June. I'm here for the school's inspection, not for a sports lesson." said a thickly accented voice followed by more *THUD*s and shuffling noises.

Mrs. June? Our gym teacher? thought Lauren as she tried in vain to free her hand. *Why is the school having some inspection? And why do I have to be such a klutz and come to the perfect place at the perfect time to perfectly mess up everything?* She shook her head and continued tugging. Seconds later, she flung out from the hidden safety of the desk and out into the open where the inspector and Mrs. June stood gawking.

"Young lady, I'd expect you to be in your class now," the inspector said as she raised an eyebrow at Mrs. June.

The gym teacher was flabbergasted as she stuttered a response. "I-I don't know h-how this could have p-possibly hap-happened," she answered.

Every action has an equal and opposite reaction, Newton's third law. At least I won't get that wrong on my science test tomorrow. But now wasn't the time for a science lesson; it was time to make up excuses. "I'm sorry, I can explain," said Lauren as she tried to come up with possible responses to give them when they asked their questions. But to her surprise, they didn't.

"How 'bout we take a nice walk to the principal's office where you can explain this, and he'll take *very* good care of you," said the inspector as she gestured toward the door.

"Um, that's not necessary right now," Lauren said as she bolted toward the door and out the school exit.

Oh no, where to go, where to go? After much apprehension, she sat down on the school playground's only bench, rustic and ancient, and thought about that cold metal thing nestled in a hole in the wall. As Lauren thought more about it, she realized she had a curiosity to find out what it was and ventured back to where she had run out of the school a few minutes before. Then she pushed the door open and entered the gymnasium with the utmost caution to find that there was no one there, thankfully.

She tiptoed into Mrs. June's office, kneeled, and felt around in the hole she had discovered earlier. And in a moment, she came in contact with the silver metal object. Lauren eased it out and quickly realized that it was a pocket watch, with intricate designs, and beautifully detailed hands. The numbers on it were extraordinarily painted with gold, and each detail was a piece of the puzzle to the entire thing itself. She turned it around and, on the back, was a large roman numeral: *XII*.

After a moment's hesitation, she was certain that this number was twelve. The significance of this watch was clear, even if Lauren knew she couldn't see it yet. Her thoughts were interrupted by the bell, and Lauren rushed out the doors and found her way to her locker. She hauled everything out of the locker and tucked the pocket watch gently into her bag. She knew she needed someone to talk with, but who? She frantically looked around for the person she knew she needed. *There!*

"Josey, come with me!" said Lauren as she grabbed her best friend's hand and took her to the old computer lab. They rushed as fast as they could, and once they were there, Lauren extracted the watch from her bag.

"A watch? That's why you dragged me here?"

Lauren told her the entire story, in great detail, with the occasional head shake or *tsk-tsk* from Josey. After Lauren had finished, Josey gently grabbed the watch from her hands and muttered, "This isn't even set right. The time is 3:25. Your watch says 5:17."

As she said this, a train whistled in the distance. With a roll of her eyes, Lauren said, "You don't know how to read time, do you? The short one is the hour hand and the longer one is the minute hand."

"Nuh-uh, *this* is how you do it," Josey said as she leaned over to get a better look at the watch in Lauren's hand and turned the little knob backward.

Lauren felt a little flutter in her stomach, and everything was quiet.

Josey gently grabbed the watch from her hands and muttered, "This isn't even set right. The time is 3:25. Your watch says 5:17."

As she said this, a train whistled in the distance. Lauren gasped.

"I-I n-need a moment." She ran to the bathroom and collapsed on the ground. Her mind was swirling with what had just happened. But there was no mistaking it: time had just turned backward.

It all started making sense now: the mystical atmosphere around the watch and the roman numeral twelve on the back. Lauren recalled from physics that twelve was the number of time and space. *I can control time!* Lauren thought. That was when Lauren started to think: *If I can move time back, can I move it forward?* She set it to 5:30, and lo and behold, she was in her bedroom with her earbuds on. *Wait, can I stop time?*

After a while, Lauren figured out how to stop time as well. All it took was a long press of the knob and she could practically hear everything freeze around her.

The downside to the watch? Well, Lauren had tried fast-forwarding to next Saturday, then rewinding to last Sunday, but it would only take her twelve hours forward and backward at the most. And stopping time only lasted for a minute, unfortunately.

This could change so much; the possibilities are endless! she mused.

The next day at school wasn't much of a day. Lauren skipped right through classes, right to lunch and recess. In less than two hours, Lauren was back home. The clock struck four and she smiled. *And to say that I completed an entire day of school in one and a half hours!* she thought, grinning. *I could get used to this!*

The next few months passed without incident until spring break rolled around. One day, in the morning, Lauren was taking a simple stroll along the lakeside, caught a glimpse of herself in the water, and gasped. Her eyes were bloodshot red, her face sunken, dark circles were under her eyes, and her hair looked like it had never seen a comb. The pocket watch

What the Dreams Whisper

was taking a toll on her, her energy slowly becoming its energy, and Lauren fast-forwarding through sleep didn't help.

"You look tired. What bothers you?" said a voice beside Lauren.

She whipped around and spotted an old man fishing. "I know your troubles, for I am the protector of the watch you behold."

Lauren's eyes widened.

"This watch is extraordinary. Did you make it, sir?"

The old man grinned and showed off his nonexistent teeth.

"Yes, it is extraordinary. Now the question is, what will you do?"

"What do you mean?"

"Will you keep it or do something else? Up to you."

Lauren sighed. She knew what she had to do. She took a deep breath and flung the watch into the crystal-clear lake. It was gone. She turned around to see what the old fisherman thought of this, but he had vanished.

The valuable lesson Lauren learned that day was that too much of anything, no matter how terrible or amazing, can still be harmful. As the great Swiss physician Paracelsus once said: "The dose makes the poison."

The Purple Shell
Myra Bisnik

"Look at this! And that! Wow!" my brother cried, nearly bursting with excitement.

We were at the beach, and I had to admit, it was one of the most beautiful ones I've ever been to. The light blue waves gently lapped the shore, occasionally revealing a colorful shell or a pearly white rock. The sun shone brightly above me, warming me down from the top of my head to the tip of my toes. The sand was soft and smooth to the touch.

"Come on, Myra!" my brother Ojas shouted, waking me from my thoughts. "Let's go to the shore!"

Before I could say anything, he dashed off toward the water. By the time I caught up, he was already bathing his legs in the ocean water.

"Come in! It's not too cold," he reassured me.

I grinned and stepped in too. It was just the right temperature. For a minute I just stood there, watching the waves come in and go out. I'd never felt this peaceful before. That is, until a huge piece of slimy seaweed came with the water and wrapped itself around my foot.

"Aaaah!" I yelled with disgust, holding up the leg with seaweed and jumping around on the other. "Gross!"

Ojas giggled and peeled off the seaweed from my leg. Then he threw it back into the water.

"Thanks," I breathed, relieved to get rid of the terrible slimy feeling.

What the Dreams Whisper

He nodded and went back to bathing his feet in the water, I took a deep breath and decided to join him, even though I was afraid I might get slimed again. I stepped into the water and looked out into the ocean, only to gasp in horror. There was a huge wave moving toward us, too fast for anyone to react. I squeezed my eyes shut. My brother let out a cry, and that was the last thing I heard before the pounding of water filled my ears.

Somehow, I was able to breathe, even when I was underwater. Then I heard Ojas's muffled voice. "Open your eyes, it's all okay!" he said happily as if nothing had happened at all.

Cautiously, I opened my eyes, expecting to see dark, murky water all around me. Instead, I saw bright, clear water and a gorgeous coral reef. Brain coral, fan coral, probably every type of coral was there! Thousands of tiny fishes were swimming around. I let out a gasp of surprise and admiration. I suddenly realized that, somehow, I was moving toward the coral reef without swimming. Curiously, I looked at my hands. There was a big bubble around each hand. The bubble seemed to be moving me forward.

"Cool!" Ojas whispered, apparently noticing the bubbles too.

After a while we arrived at the reef. The big bubbles had dissolved into the water, so I could move around freely. Just then, at least fifty tiny bubbles came flying out of nowhere and joined together to make one big bubble. The bubble made the shape of a boy about my age. I could not believe my eyes. But I was even more surprised when the boy suddenly started talking.

"Hello," the boy said, in a rather hurried tone. "I am sorry. There is no time to explain now. All I can tell you is that I can control bubbles. You have to come with me." At that, he waved his hands and the big bubbles appeared again around our arms. They started pulling Ojas and I toward the heart of the reef. The bubble boy glided along beside us. I was about to ask him where we were going and who he was, but before I could even open my mouth, we stopped at the reef. The bubble boy started to explain everything. "You see, I have heard a lot about you two," he began. "You have helped so many people. The reef is in trouble so I hope you could help us too."

Ojas was the first to speak. "Sure! What is the trouble?" he asked, glad to have another person to help. The bubble boy swam aside to reveal a beautiful pedestal. It seemed to be made of gold. Intricate designs had been engraved into the pedestal. But the pedestal was not the most interesting object there. It was what was on the pedestal. It was a gorgeous purple conch shell. It shimmered a thousand colors when the light hit it.

"This is the Shell of Infinity," said the bubble boy. "It reflects the sunlight coming through the water, creating an invisible protective force field around this coral reef. But lately, because of the trash that comes into the water, the water becomes murky, and the sunlight can't come through. Plus, when fish swallow the trash, they get sick." He pointed upward.

I looked up and realized that there were floating plastic bags, crumpled up plastic bottles, and stray fishing nets. The water was slightly murky and blocked the sunlight out. I suddenly felt sorry for all these creatures having to live in this dirty water. I thought for a few minutes and came up with a plan.

"We can help you," I said confidently, "we just need to go to the surface."

The bubble boy nodded and gestured the bubbles around our arms to go up to the surface. We immediately started shooting back up to the surface, and after a few minutes, we were above the ocean's waves.

"Come on!" Ojas cried and started to swim toward the shore.

I joined him. Soon, we were at the sandy shore of the beach. I explained my plan to Ojas and he nodded with agreement.

We both clambered up a high rock on the beach. "Everybody!" I yelled. "We need your help!"

Soon a small group of kids gathered around to hear what I had to say.

"The coral reef needs our help. We need to go and clean up all the trash there," I explained loudly and clearly. "So are you ready to help?"

There was a cry of agreement from the crowd, and they all started running toward the shore.

"Nice speech!" Ojas said.

I grinned and we started running toward the shore with the rest of the group. I explained to them that we'd be able to breath and move underwater. We all dived in at the same time. As soon as we went inside the water, bubbles formed around our hands and started pulling us toward the beautiful coral reef.

When we reached the coral reef, the bubble boy was there, waiting for us. He waved his arms, and the bubbles around our hands turned into bubble nets. A few people let out gasps of surprise. The bubble boy winked at me, and I nodded back.

"All right! Let's clean up all this garbage!" I instructed.

All the kids started swimming around, catching all the trash in their bubble nets. About an hour later, all the trash had been collected. The water seemed clearer, and the sunlight was filtering through easily.

"Thank you. Thank you so much!" the bubble boy told us gratefully. "I won't forget this. Goodbye!"

Before any of us had the chance to say goodbye back, he turned into a thousand tiny bubbles and disappeared. Suddenly, the bubble nets we were holding turned back into bubbles and covered our arms. Then, they started moving toward the surface, taking us along with them.

As we were gliding back to the surface, I had some time to think. I remembered how I had been so uncomfortable because of the seaweed around my leg. Then, I thought about the poor fishes having to live in such dirty water. The seaweed couldn't harm me, though, and I had still gotten so troubled over it. It made me realize how difficult it must have been for sea creatures to live in that polluted environment. Suddenly it dawned on me that this was just a beginning and not an end. There are many more oceans to clean and many more sea creatures to help.

Finally, we reached the surface of the water. Everyone scrambled onto the sandy seashore, chatting excitedly about the adventure. The warm sun's glow felt good after being in cold water. I felt happy and proud that I helped so many

What the Dreams Whisper

fishes. I realized that I could change the world by ensuring sea creatures lived in a clean environment. I would spread awareness to recycle more and use less plastic, so it didn't end up in the in the ocean and cause harm. I also realized something Ojas and I had learned today: to always watch out for big waves on the beach!

Only the Purest
Tina Zhao

When there is someone at the door at three in the morning, it's never something good.

Nevaeh Heaven's eyes swiftly flickered open as she heard the sharp sound of the doorbell. Eighteen years old, she lived with only her mother, who worked nights. Her father and brother had died in a car crash when she was ten, suddenly gone, forever.

Nevaeh quickly rolled out of bed, groaning as her bare feet pressed down on the cold wooden floor. She scampered down the stairs and opened the front door, to find a police officer standing awkwardly on the doorstep.

"Is this the Heaven family home? I wonder, could I come in…?"

"Of course. What happened ?" Nevaeh asked, but she could already sense from the way the policeman stood there, unable to make eye contact and miserable, his tone sorrowful and bitter.

It was three thirty. Her mother had died at work from a heart attack. Nevaeh was now completely alone, at home. The world was ghost-quiet; she could almost *smell* the silent air. Perhaps this was the hour, the night hour, she had read about in a fantasy story. After lying motionless on her bed, Nevaeh decided everything had to be better in the morning.

This might all be a dream… When I open my eyes, I will find my mother calling me for breakfast…

Nevaeh's eyes shut once more and she slowly drifted off to sleep…

Nevaeh rubbed her eyes open. She felt something hot under her, like…*sand!*

She looked around. The blazing sun cast its rays on the smooth but weathered rocks by the seaside. The shimmering waves charged ashore, rattling the tiny pebbles, as if nudging them. Nevaeh was on a beach. *This is madness! I'm on a beach suddenly, but where?*

Images of her playing happily with her mom and dad on the beach flashed into her mind.

Nevaeh flickered her gaze to her right. There was a small bottle on the sand, and inside it was a note. It was rusty and old, but was somehow communicating with her, as if the bottle was pulling her nearer it. With an irresistible urge to open the bottle, she lifted herself up and tottered unsteadily toward it. She twisted the corroded cap and finally opened it with huge effort, when it made a soft popping sound. Her eyes glowed with pride. *I've never been able to force a bottle open before. I was always too weak. Let alone a tight, old, and rusty bottle.*

She unfolded the note, and it said:

Dear Nevaeh,

This is from your family. The reason all of us died was because of a curse. Our ancestors did something unforgivable to anger the Gods, so they cast a spell and only the purest heart in the family can break this curse. We now ask you, Nevaeh, our only hope left, to find the Gods and get the gem of forgiveness and love. We brought you to this realm because we believe this is the world where you will find the gem. Go toward the sunset. It will be your guide. When you face problems, open this note. Do not mourn us. We will always be at your side and may heaven light up your path, Nevaeh Heaven.

Nevaeh frowned and blinked in disbelief. All of this came to Nevaeh like a bolt from the blue, and she felt stunned. As she stood up, she tumbled back down because her legs were like noodles. But then she felt determined, thinking of her mother's warm amber gaze and her father's icy, though loving blue eyes. Despite all the worry and questions she had, her family's fate lay on her shoulders.

She carefully filled the bottle with sea water. Wasting no time, she headed toward the direction of the setting sun. Her great adventure had begun.

She had been walking for several hours without any food or drinkable water. *Or had it been half a day?* Nevaeh didn't know anymore. She was so exhausted she sat down on a small rock to rest, scanning the scene; she was not on a beach anymore. She was in a parched meadow. Nevaeh didn't feel safe in such an open area. She preferred woodland with trees protecting her. *Am I asking too much? No, I didn't even ask for any of this!*

As Nevaeh thought in frustration, she saw a well nearby. She stood up, walked over hesitantly, and peeked inside excitedly, but her face darkened. The well was empty. She stared into the darkness while her throat and lips dried. Nevaeh removed the note from her pocket—the previous words had faded away. It said now: *In the dark, hope and positivity will light up the sky.*

Nevaeh felt she understood this riddle.

What the Dreams Whisper

I hope I can have water; no, I know I will have water. I am going to restore the gem in the mountain and go back home safely, Nevaeh thought firmly.

Just at this heartbeat, water bubbled and rose up the well. Nevaeh scrambled from the shade of the well to the bucket hanging down and brought fresh water up. She dunked her bottle into the water and drank delightedly. *It tastes sweeter than usual, probably because I earned it,* Nevaeh thought with satisfaction.

She continued her journey, venturing into a rainforest. The combined scent of soil, moisture, and rain was not unpleasant; it was the smell of life. The trees' leaves were a rich, dark green, with a waxy coating, and mangoes dangled nearby. Nevaeh took one and slowly pressed it to her lips; the sweet, pulpy scent got the better of her. She took a mouthful of the ripe fruit, sweet juice dripping from her lips.

Just as Nevaeh was about to take another bite, she heard a rustle. She turned her head in the direction of the sound, and a pair of amber eyes stared at her—a tiger. It carried a pungent musky odor when it padded slowly toward Nevaeh, bared its teeth, and dug its sharp claws into the ground. Sensing further danger, Nevaeh looked over her shoulders; sure enough, a second tiger.

Neaveh expected death, but an idea suddenly came to her. She reached down to her pocket again, unfolding the note. The words had faded, like last time and cursive handwriting slowly appeared:

The tigers are thriving and are not angry in winter without prey because comfort music is prey.

What does this mean? Music is not prey! Nevaeh couldn't waste any more time; a second of thinking, a second closer to death. She guessed that the tigers were angry because she took their precious food. But prey according to the note isn't food—it's *music*.

Nevaeh didn't want to think anymore. *It's now, or never!*

She began to sing a lullaby that her mother sang to her whenever she was upset. The tigers magically sheathed their claws and let their fur lay flat down their shoulders. They weren't so scary after all. Nevaeh let out a sigh of relief and kept on with her adventure.

Nevaeh was now walking up a hill, a hiking path, almost as if it was meant for her. The sun was just setting, and the sky was a gradient of purple-orange. As Nevaeh's heart melted before the beautiful sight, somehow it restored peace and happiness for her, but she was not paying attention to her path. She suddenly slipped and fell into a crevasse. The sunset light dimmed as she fell, and she closed her eyes and accepted her fate. *I never thought I would die by falling…*

Suddenly, Nevaeh hit the ground with a loud thump, but she was miraculously alive! All she could see was a giant withered tree. "Hello? Who are you? Is there actually *someone* here?"

All of a sudden, a voice came from the tree: "Who dares to overstep their mortal authority!"

"My name is Nevaeh Heaven. I've come from far away to plead with you to stop the curse that you cast on our family!"

"They deserve it!"

"What did we even do?"

"Ha, do you know why those tigers are so protective of a small batch of mango? Or why everything looks dried up?"

Nevaeh thought for a second. Then her eyes widened in surprise.

In a moment, a mist swarmed around Nevaeh, and she was shivering—the air was as cold as the winter night. Then a sickly lady appeared in front of her as the mist cleared. She was pale and had a wide, round face with a pointed chin. Her silver hair was straight, silky, but unhealthy, and her dark emerald eyes were almond-shaped. She was wearing a dark brown empire dress.

"If you want to break the curse, find the gem and restore it in the tree behind me," whispered the lady. "By the way, my name is Mother Nature." She vanished.

Nevaeh had no clue where she should start looking for the gem, so she opened the note once more. Now it only said: *Pure flowing water.*

She knew immediately and darted past the tree to reach the waterfall, Mediterranean-blue and clear; she could even see her own reflection on the surface.

Nevaeh heard a wonderful singing voice, coming from under the waterfall's flowing water. She saw a crystal-clear gem. *This must be it!*

Nevaeh quickly fished the gem out of the water and immediately felt the purity of it. She turned her head and ran toward the heart of the tree, carefully placing the fragile gem in the tree, which spontaneously lit up. She could see heavenly rays shining from above and warm rain showering down. As her vision blurred, a whisper from her mother rang in Nevaeh's ears: *"Thank you…"*

This is Nevaeh, a forty-year-old successful writer married to a doctor, with two kids. They live a happy, safe, and fruitful life.

Hawaii

Boris Cheung

Summer 1941

A window creaked open on the stone face of a Shanghai *shikumen*, disturbing its anxious silence. It was sunset. A filthy subtropical mist hung over the occupied city. It could've choked the azure-winged magpies that flew low, looking for gold.

A black figure whisked through the building, dropping lightly onto its battered ground floor. The Chinese man, his eyes shadowed by a trilby hat, padded up to the safe with long, slow steps, like a walking palm in the heat. After a series of insectoid ticks, it cracked open, and the spy grasped a brown envelope as he wondered when the Japanese occupants would return.

But let's allow the spy to tell the story for himself. The Americans called him Astley.

***

Slipping back into the depths of the city, I found a concealed concrete cove where I awaited further instructions. Now I was to help the Americans get info on the Japanese— in return for a handsome paycheck. My stomach rumbled like a motor. The Japanese had been ravaged and the food they had stolen was barely enough to live on.

Suddenly, I heard a small creak in the ground. I spun my head as I saw a figure sit up from a velvet-cushioned chair, left to sit regally in ruins—

A Japanese spy slowly extended his long white arm in the moonlight and aimed a Nambu pistol at me.

Scrambling onto the rubble, I shuddered onto my feet, and a sharp pain skimmed the soft tissue of my shoulder. I smelled metal, and blood trickled out.

I instinctively plunged forward, grabbed the handle of the pistol, and disarmed the spy. We pulled each other to the ground beneath the window's light, throwing fists in the darkness. With one hook, I bruised his head, and it hit the stone floor with a crunch. The whites of his open eyes drained of life in the dark.

I wasted no time. Covering my bleeding shoulder, I ran out the front door and proceeded with my mission.

Under cover from a silvery fog and a relentless storm, I wearily limped to an isolated part of the peninsula on a tributary of the Yangtze River and, just as planned, found a small rowing boat carrying weapon supplies in case of capture.

***

Within hours, I met a military attaché, Percival, from the US Embassy, in a safehouse, and handed him a long piece of tape with the following message:

NISHINAS TEST WORKED STOP FUEL FOR MORE SUFFICIENT STOP JAPS PLAN KILLING BLOW IN CHINA OR PACIFIC STOP EITHER OR BOTH IMMINENT STOP PREVENT NOW STOP REPLY FAST STOP CONFIRMATION NEEDED STOP

Percival stood beneath a fan in the nondescript trading office. And for a moment, all I heard was its little whirr.

What the Dreams Whisper

Drained, he slowly removed his cap and sat in a skeletal chair. His desert-brown shirt looked corpselike in the dim light, and he had to close his eyes for a moment.

Doctor Yoshio Nishina finally had a nuclear weapon.

"Astley, your contact's information is…invaluable. It demands a quick and careful response from us. I'll report back to my superiors. I've got your payment here—and *stay in contact*. We've never needed each other more."

***

After trudging through the scorched terrain, I encountered a small Japanese detachment from a garrison in the area, milling around in a covered courtyard like thieves. As I walked briskly by them, I slid a neatly folded envelope into an open chest by the boots of an officer with his back turned to me.

OPERATION TORCH PLANNED TO CUT OFF JAPAN FROM SUPPLIERS AND DESTROY PRODUCTION STOP WILL END ALL JAP OPS IF IT WORKS STOP PREEMPTIVE STRIKE NEEDED STOP

***

The city behind me was choked with barbed wire. I walked beyond its control points in a long zigzag, then emerged like a hermit crab near a lonely, boarded-up inn surrounded by trucks and carts.

As I slammed open its door, I was greeted by walls splashed with bright red banners and stars and the beady eyes of its guerilla occupants.

I embraced Lin, their leader. A forester from the country's heart, he was out of his natural habitat here, but his big, leathery face evinced cunning and bravery. He greeted me softly.

"Hu, my brother, welcome home. You're playing the *guqin* for your best audience ever here! What information do you have?"

My tired eyes roved over a military document file, marked with the Imperial seal. It was a tightly held prisoner in his calloused hands. They still smelled oily, like cordite. It read:

THE MILITARY IS GOING SOUTH TO NEUTRALIZE THE AIRFIELDS STOP AIM TO PREVENT MORE RAIDS ON JAPAN AND MERCHANT SHIPS STOP

Before anyone could react to the news, the weak wooden door to the house splintered and burst open. A unit of Japanese soldiers shoved their Arisaka rifles through the new hole and fired on the mass of humanity inside. There was chaos, and the air itself, not only the banners, was now stained with red mist.

Yelling, Lin drew his pistol and dived behind a table, throwing it over. Steel tore into the bodies of a couple of Japanese, and they slammed shut like penknives and keeled over. But the Chinese were also falling like flies.

I stormed through the back door under a storm of Japanese and Chinese fire and escaped into the nearby village, where I planned to make my final move. The growing conflict was partly unleashed by me. Now I was to nip it in the bud.

***

What the Dreams Whisper

With a new Japanese document in my hand, I followed the sirenlike wail of an American propaganda trumpet to the US Concession.

I scaled a stone wall blocking an alleyway circling the US Consulate General—not as difficult as you might imagine. Guards were thin on the ground, as the Americans were thinking of leaving. My little nuclear message had perhaps sped that along. But first, they were no doubt trying to corroborate it. More time bought for me.

Dropping lightly into a yellowing patch of grass by the imposing stone face of the embassy, I could practically feel the Americans' panic in the air. I made my way through a service door and padded softly up a carpeted stairway. The corridors were filled with men frantically diving from one door to another and ringing telephones. I attracted little attention.

Finally I reached Percival's office and knocked. In barking cadences, he invited me in.

I was surprised. Not that the curtains were drawn. Not that Percival was sitting behind his desk. But that his voice was a disciplined rumble rather than a defeated whisper. He waved at the comfiest armchair, facing the fireplace.

Half encouraged and half perplexed, I sat, gazing at a half-played chess game abandoned at the feet of my armchair. I reclined hatless, listening to Percival pouring us drinks behind me.

"I've been in discussions about your intelligence."

Blunt. No emotion betrayed. He stirred ice in the glass.

"I'm glad you returned. I have work for you."

Footsteps. The fireplace, like the mouth of a black beast, sat empty in front of me.

"Drink up," he said, handing me a whisky glass as he stepped in front of my armchair.

He didn't wait to sit down. We both drank up instead, and he looked at me curiously.

Satiated, I finally spoke. "I'm at your disposal—"

And Percival pulled out his ivory-grip Colt .45, pointing it right at my upper chest.

"Absolutely. Why else would we let you waltz back in here?"

I breathed a little more heavily. My hands instinctively reached out slowly from me, but I was trapped in the armchair. "Percival, you're making a mistake."

"We know you're feeding us Jap misinformation. What are they paying you, Astley? More than your own damn country is worth?"

Percival inched a little closer, his aim steady.

"I was thinking of extracting more info from you. But when I think about how you've tried to intimidate us—with lies—the consequences for the Pacific—do you even realize that Washington might *attack*, not get out of Asia?" His voice, finally shaking a little, once again cooled. "Then I think: it's been a good run for you."

Before I had time to get up, Percival was distracted by a thin band of white light over his body, his eye—

A muffled gunshot. And Percival dropped like an angel in the white flame of the half-open door, one eye socket torn out by a bullet.

Shaking, I turned slowly around, looking over the armchair.

What the Dreams Whisper

"Nakamura." A man in a raincoat, his face a little skeletal with its high cheekbones, grunted from the now-closing door, shaking a little smoke out of his silenced pistol. "Japanese intelligence. And you, Astley, have a lot to thank me for. I'm a sleeper agent here, and I know you're not. Start talking. What information about our future operations have you given them?"

There was a beat. Standing slowly, I realized I had to seem to have a story that satisfied everyone. *Delay first.* I stepped toward him.

"HAWAII—"

I shoved my hand into his face without thinking—my glass still in my hand. It shattered. With a howl of pain, Nakamura dropped his pistol and collapsed, clutching his bleeding face.

Leave him here. Let the Americans deal with him. Thankfully, I had the foresight to grab a nice golden watch from Percival's desk, though, as I opened the window and jumped out.

Speeding along an alleyway outside, I melted into the city, as the embassy screamed with bells and gunshots.

But not before I composed a new message for brother Lin in my head:

JAPS SCARED OF US STOP NEITHER SIDE UNDERSTANDS SITUATION STOP PREEMPTIVE STRIKE BY ONE SEEMS LIKELY BY DECEMBER STOP

A Storm in Heaven

Clarence Yim

I slowly lifted my head from the sand. One side of my face burned like leather, feeling thick, heavy and lined with hot, salty dust. Some of my skin had not only burned but seemed molten into an alien new shape, angry blood bubbling up beneath it like lava.

It was 1935. My plane had suddenly crashed down into an island, with hot sand blanketing the ground, bleached by scorching sunlight.

I was the only body to awaken. I jumped down from the wreckage, clutching a parachute and my backpack, and moved away as the great plane burned.

I wandered, lonely, on the island, surrounded by oceans full of hungry sharks. Miserably, I sat down onto the soft sand for just a minute, then retrieved a fishing rod from the plane.

I tried fishing. The clear water showed a gray dot, foggy, with the left side moved and moved, fighting for freedom. Just freedom.

It wiggled as I took the hook up, twisting and turning its strong body. It struggled, refusing to surrender. But it was too late. Too late.

My hands were trembling. I pulled hard, tugging the fish out of the water. Its gray scales, glistening in the shimmering sunlight, showed up.

I took out a lighter and lit some teak, starting a fire. My blue eyes darted around, quickly, looking for snakes.

Every small step kicked up a cloud of sand.

A cobra struck out of nowhere.

It slithered in the golden sand, pushing toward me—

I took out my Swiss Army knife, opened the knife, and threw it at the snake—

It chopped off its tail. The snake slithered away, shocked.

I went near the fire, and my body shivered. Hard.

The weather was cold. The sounds of *crack*s accompanied me for the whole night, with enormous rocks breaking into two.

I roasted the fish and ate it, with fresh seawater as salt. Then I went fishing—

And a yacht came by.

A middle-aged man sat inside, holding a fishing rod.

The yacht stopped.

The man shouted, "Can I live here? My yacht ran out of fuel!"

I agreed.

The man came up and introduced himself. "I'm James, an American, and I am here because my yacht broke down. Can I stay here?"

I nodded. I met my best friend who rode through high, rough waves and low, gentle waves with me, my best companion.

I started the campfire while James caught some fish with the shrimp inside his yacht. It was hard, but nothing could stop us.

James caught a lot of fish I couldn't identify. They glimmered like silver on the grill.

***

"My name is Norman Nathan. I come from Brownsville, NYC. I was returning from a business trip, back to New York. But my plane crashed."

"I was living on the ship, searching for things to survive. But I ran out of fuel too fast."

"Why are you living in a boat?"

He shrugged, his eyes staring right ahead like little black beads. "It's how I live. I'm not...materialistic. It's a houseboat."

"Where do you come from?"

He frowned and glared at the sea, though only for a split second. "San Francisco. Nothing special. Look at that tree, there's a cute bulbul. How's your family? I mean, contact...?"

I struggled to put on a smile. "Okay."

***

One day, when I was looking for soil and veggie seeds, I stepped on the boat for the first time. Inside I found some seeds and a trunk. I opened it with a heavy golden key and inside was silvery white platinum.

James suddenly appeared as I closed the trunk.

He barked, "What are you doing here?"

I responded. "Just looking for the shrimp."

He said, "I can do it."

Looking gently but firmly at me, he herded me out.

A cool, dark night. Captain Laurence lightly brushed his white coat, whistled a happy tune, and placed the heavy brass telescope onto his dark gray eye. On the flat horizon, a sandy island, and men as small as ants were flashing a light into the dark sky—

SOS, in Morse code.

I piloted the ship to them.

Under the shimmering moonlight, two men were perched on the shore as if shocked little birds.

I inflated a rescue ship and sailed the little boat into the embrace of the soft white sand.

They talked, looking at each other with bloodred eyes.

I said, "Don't worry, men. I will help you out of the situation." I continued, "By the way, why are you guys in this sad situation?"

One man replied, "Oh, 'cause I was taking a trip through the Pacific, but my fuel ran out."

The other man shouted, "What? You said you were living on the ship five months ago!"

The man tried not to meet the other's eyes as he mumbled, "I mean, I was…"

"Okay, please climb aboard. We are going back to the ship. I will give you food and also a telephone to contact your family."

***

Within a few days, after nibbling on tasty biscuits and drinking hot tea, Captain Laurence finally broached the topic again. They had been as distant as Charon. "Would you like to contact your family by telephone?"

"Oh, thanks! I will call my family," one said.

I then asked the other man. "How about you?"

The other man replied, "Oh, I have no one to contact. I am not married."

Captain Laurence was suspicious and said, "You don't have a family?"

The other man's fists clenched as they rested on the hot metal table, and he blinked slowly.

"Hold on! You said that your family was okay five months ago!"

The other man replied, "Oh, I don't have my father and mother, but I have my grandparents."

I brought them into a room, where two telephones sat on the table.

"Call your families," I said with a smile.

"No need. Don't worry about me."

***

Morning. The endless blue sky of the Pacific summer had given way to the mottled gray mists of the Bay Area, shrouding the thick red Golden Gate Bridge. Winds howled a little more shrilly, as they slammed into the cliff faces of the West Coast. The ship snaked along the coastline and into the harbor. Its strange occupants both looked overboard, smiling weakly, their hands gripping rusting rails. Then one of them quietly slipped away, his narrow feet barely making a sound on the metal walkways and stairs.

They arrived in San Francisco, and the customs gate, red and blaring warnings, began to loom over them, when—

The coast guard stopped the man cold.

The sailor took out his fist and punched the guard, with one long curve, in his stomach.

He keeled over, face contorted with pain.

The sailor was ready to fight.

Suddenly, with a wicked smile, the sailor dropped his duffel bag, took out a sword, and swung it mechanically, like a torturer's pendulum.

The coast guard's head fell off.

***

A white horse stood in the warm sunlight, basking in coast guard green outside the federal gate. Shoving aside the stunned crowd, I kicked open the exit door, and I mounted it, as bells and tortured faces, like white petals in the black crowd, began to scream behind me, arms waving like wheat.

It kicked off—then galloped at full speed. *North.*

Just as I rounded a city corner, the smell of the sea dying behind me, gunshots finally smacked into the brick, hurling red dust.

***

As the bloodred California sun set over Marin County, the murderer dived over a grassy hilltop's lip, burrowing behind the exposed roots of a cut-down tree. His eyes, alert but cold, glanced back at SF only once. His chest heaved, but like any sailor, he could control his nausea and his breathing pretty well. The cops' bells, jangling from boxy cars and blue telephone boxes, and the screams of bystanders had waned behind him as his thin boots pounded first pavements, then hills. *America—but not back inside.*

Turning back to his duffel bag, now stained with someone else's blood, he cleaned his blade on the thick grass and stashed it inside. As he unzipped it, a crinkled little brown passport—decades old—winked at him from the top of the pile of weapons glinting inside.

Robert Rickerts.

Time to head north. I'm not going back to Alcatraz.

Damn those new buddies of mine. I help one out, and it gets me help I don't want.

Last time I try to be good…

***

Five days after returning home, I went for a checkup. Two hours seemed like two decades long.

The doctor said, "Sorry, sir. You have skin cancer. Surgery is an option…or we can offer you palliative care."

I could only nod.

***

Inside the dark surgery room, the doctor inserted a scalpel in my chest, cutting a half-moon. It bled hard. But I had to survive…

***

I had to stay at the hospital. One bright morning, I secretly sneaked out of the hospital, and ran home where I wrote my will:

I, George Washington, will give my house, money, and everything to my dearest son, Frederick Washington.

Suddenly, my eyes fell on the diary. I opened it, and on the first page wrote:

I must never let my son, George Washington, know that I am a killer. I must pretend to be a good mom.

I shivered. I placed the diary back and dashed to the hospital.

***

Back in the hospital, the nurse touched my icy hand, and with her slippery white glove, wrote scratchily: *George Washington. Breathing ceased 20:18.*

My relatives waved me goodbye and sobbed as I closed my eyes.

Give It a Chance
Harini Nachiappan

It was around midnight in my new home. I absolutely hated it here. For the time we had been here, I'd been hearing strange noises from the basement, and I just felt uneasy; like something—no—*someone* was watching.

Dad had gotten a promotion and we had had to move to Springfield. For the past twelve years of my life, I had lived in Greenville. I loved it there, and the best part was that I had so many friends. Now, there was this unsettling idea in the back of my head that I would have to start all over again.

As I tossed and turned in bed, I felt a soft breeze against my skin, and I tried burying myself in the covers.

Not working.

I got up and saw a flamy plum-purple glowing beacon wandering loftily in the hallway. It stopped, beckoning me to follow. I shivered.

Should I follow it or not? I figured I'd go and check it out, since I wasn't getting any sleep either way.

I was in my panda-face blue onesie as I tiptoed past my parents' room to the steps and slowly crept downstairs. Just as I came down, I saw the glow enter the basement.

I chased after it. When I arrived, the beacon was hovering near an antique bookcase. My mom had bought it from a thrift shop with a few books in it.

It motioned to an old, heavy brown book and I pulled it out. Just as I flipped it open, the purple light plunged through the pages and a pale lavender cloud of dust swirled up noiselessly, sucking everything in sight through.

***

I stumbled and realized I was no longer in the basement. The first thing I noticed was that it was morning. I was outside a forest in front of something similar to a palace, with a long, white bridge. The palace was a creamy beige color, and the turrets were all rosy-pink.

My mind was racing. The plan was to find a friendly person and ask them how to get back home. Then I could call the police and they would take me home. It was as simple as that—or it was supposed to be.

The center of the palace had wooden double doors with four guards. I was wondering if I should ask the guards when I saw a girl riding a beautiful palomino horse in a field of lavender. She was wearing a sandy-pink gown with sleeves made of sheer lace and golden glittery flecks all over. Her hair was a brunette-red mix and went halfway down her back, styled in a French braid.

I followed her to the edge of a river. She reared the horse and jumped off to face me, hearing my footsteps.

"Who are you? Why are you following me?" she asked. She held her arms out, as if to defend herself. She was about two and a half inches taller than me.

"I'm Hannah. I'm from Springfield. I got sucked through a book and ended up here. I'm looking for a way back home," I said. The sentence sounded weird on my tongue.

"I …" She trailed off, passing a questioning look at me and looking around. She sighed and sacked me over the horse, riding me to who-knows-where.

A few minutes later, she dropped me down in the middle of the forest.

"Hey. I'm Princess Ainsley of the Eastern Kingdom of Magic, daughter of Queen Adele and King Arwen. There is also a Western Kingdom of Magic, and we have a long-time feud with them. I'm on surveillance because of that. And I think I know how to help you," she whispered.

She whistled a high-pitched tune at frequencies I shouldn't have been able to hear. My ears rang for a few minutes. Then I heard wings flapping. Two oversize monarch butterflies flew down to the ground, landing with a soft thump. They left golden trails of dust in the air.

I was mesmerized by the paranormal flamy orange and yellow butterfly wings, when I heard Ainsley talk.

"Get on. I'll explain everything later."

She had a demanding voice, and I did as I was told. I was struggling to get on when the butterfly bent back helpfully.

"My name's Roxy. Welcome to our world!" exclaimed the enthusiastic young butterfly in an uncanny voice. She—it could talk! I was so confused.

Very soon, I realized that Ainsley was not the army general I thought she was, and was in fact a very kind and friendly person.

I also learned that I was in a new mystical world, and it was unheard of to travel between worlds if not helped by a rare pixie, and that the creature I was riding on was called a Sommious Butter Dragon. *That* was when I noticed its wings had scales.

I tried to take in the glorious view and take my mind off the problems at hand. Mountains upon mountains, cities, and ant-size people took up most of the view, cluttered with graceful, puffy clouds.

We crossed a border and I felt a jolt. We were now in the Neutral Islands of Magic. This was where havoc was halted.

We crossed a large stony-faced mountain and landed in front of Café Chaos. We walked in. Suddenly, we were on the ceiling, sitting on teal-blue couches, curved behind a corner table. All the blood rushed to my brain.

The restaurant had gleaming checkered black-and-white tiles, paired with pale yellow walls. The tabletops were a yellowish wood color with black fancy stands. There was a very loud marching parade on the floor that had seemed to fall out of control, leaving the members running loose like chickens. It was…chaotic. My head was pounding.

"Order please!" shouted a waiter from below.

Or I think it was a waiter? He looked more like a single stand table with floppy black beams for arms and a talking bowl of tomato red soup for his head.

"I want a buffalo latte, a seaweed doughnut…and oyster soup?" she ordered.

I realized that the descriptions of the food items were completely different from the names of the foods, AND the print was in a different language!

"Also, add an Unquenchable Bag." She glanced over at me and winked. I gave her a thankful smile.

"Of course." The waiter bowed and left.

The café was very busy with ogres, talking turnips, thirsty vampires, and krakens. A few moments later, the waiter came back with our food on a black twisty cart.

There was a classic cheeseburger, waffle fries, croissants, a bean burrito, and churros. Best of all was the heavenly mouth-melting chocolate! I tuned into the jazzy music and gazed at the shimmery glass chandeliers.

***

After our scrumptious meal and a few good laughs, we got back to my mess. She told me that the only being she knew who could possibly help me lived at Whitgarde—a fancy manor in an urban town by the name of Bellwood.

Ainsley and I left the restaurant and flew our way to Whitgarde. We passed more shops along the way and stopped a few times!

It was magical. My favorites were Griffins 'n Gargoyles, the Wise Cauldron, the Summoning Scroll, and the Hourglass.

Eventually, we made our way toward Whitgarde again, but this time, with bags of goodies.

"Pixie Daphne lives at Whitgarde, one of the last pixies left. She's the only pixie I know who might be willing to help you," Ainsley explained.

"But what if she can't—or worse, won't—help me?" I blurted out.

I got no response.

***

We knocked upon the heavy brown doors of Whitgarde, and a butler let us in. We sat down just as a dark-skinned pixie with a beautiful purple and white gradient frock came floating down the dark brown wooden steps.

She greeted us with a warm smile. "Welcome! I have been expecting you for quite a while, Hannah. Good day, Ainsley." She had a sharp, stern voice. Ainsley gave a slight bow.

"Daphne? You look so familiar…" I trailed off, trying to place her in my mind.

She gave a small laugh. "Of course! That's because I am the light you saw in your house. I have been watching your family for the past three days, and you seemed quite…miserable. Ask me whatever you want. I know you have questions." Daphne smiled mischievously.

"Okay…why did you bring me here?" I asked her curiously.

Daphne snapped her fingers.

Suddenly Ainsley vanished, and I heard wings flapping.

"Well…every world has its own beauty…" She trailed off.

"So…you want me to give Springfield a chance?" I asked her blandly.

"Every world has its own shine, no matter how glorious or downright dusky. You just need to see Springfield in a new light," Daphne said in a cryptic voice.

I paused to wonder what she meant. "I guess I could give it a chance. Why is it so important I stay in Springfield?" I asked her.

Suddenly I heard my mother's voice, and my alarm clock ringing in the background.

"Because—" She paused, hearing the noises. "Oops! Your time's up! Remember what I said, Hannah. You have better things ahead of you. Goodbye!" Daphne snapped her fingers, and her smile fell away.

I woke up in bed, with my mom trying to wake me up and turn off my blaring alarm at the same time.

Today, I was going to set sail in new waters. I was going to give Springfield the chance it needed.

The Fruit of Endurance
Saira Thomas

The three of us stood in the smoldering sun beholding the same banner, but the emotions coursing through each one of us were quite varied.

"CONGRATULATIONS JACK FOR WINNING YOUR 50TH AWARD!" screamed the yellow banner in front of our home in bright red letters along with a smiling snapshot of Jack with his medals and trophies.

Jack wore a wide grin on his face.

"Don't be so smug!" Jeremy grumbled.

"I'm just four awards away."

I wish I could say, "Beware, I'm not so far behind either! Unfortunately…"

All three of us brothers shared the same physical features—tall, lean, wavy strawberry-blonde hair, and turquoise eyes—but the similarities ended there! Jack, the eldest, was the athlete of the family, excelling in all sorts of sports. And Jeremy, the youngest, was the "brains" of the family, excelling in academics.

And I was the middle brother who excelled at…nothing in particular. I was the boring average Joe who never won any awards however hard I tried. While my brothers went out for competitions and fancy trainings, I helped my parents with household chores. I didn't grudge my brothers their success, but I yearned for my hard work to bear fruit!

"Kiddos!"

I was pulled out of my self-depreciating thoughts by a cheerful, booming voice.

"Grandpa!"

All three of us sprinted toward Grandpa's open arms.

Grandpa had come to take us to his home for summer vacation. We loved spending time at Grandpa's country house. Jack, being the daredevil, enjoyed swimming in the lake and climbing as many trees as he wished. Jeremy enjoyed sitting outside in the calm and quiet and reading to his heart's content. I loved that I could relax and forget about not being so special.

Grandpa, just like my parents, never compared me with my brothers. He always tried to convince me that putting in an honest day's work was just as important.

It was later that night after finishing dinner at Grandpa's home that he dropped the bomb on us. "You better go to bed early so that you can be at the zoo at seven," Grandpa said.

All of us looked up at him, puzzled.

"Ah! Did I forget to mention that I have signed you up for volunteer work at the zoo? It's just for two hours every morning for three weeks," explained Grandpa.

Jack immediately perked up. "OOH! I wouldn't mind working with some tigers and lions. This is so cool! My friends are going to be so jealous!" He started typing furiously on his phone.

My eyes also lit up because I really loved animals and birds even though I was not very confident about caring for tigers and lions.

The next day morning promptly at seven, Grandpa dropped us off at the zoo and drove off after promising to be back on time to pick us up.

Bill, the manager of the zoo, greeted us enthusiastically at his office. "You guys will be taking care of our exotic birds. You can feed them and pet them like they're your own. Here is the list of your duties and instructions on how to care for each bird! You can come to me if you've any doubts."

"Sooooo…no lions or tigers," Jack murmured, disappointed, passing the list to me.

Jeremy sported his usual nonchalant face. I for one was ecstatic! I adored birds and it was a dream come true.

"Oh! And here are your uniform shirts." Bill handed each of us a bright yellow shirt with *ZOOKEEPER* written on the front and *VOLUNTEER* on the back and also the zoo's emblem on the sleeves. We all quickly donned the shirts and got to work.

As days passed, I bonded with all the macaws, hornbills, toucans, cockatoos, parakeets, lovebirds, and so on and also started learning more about them. I toiled away cleaning up the cages, changing the water, and filling up their food while Jeremy assisted me in sorting out the food for each species. He was not very keen on going near the birds so he spent the rest of the time reading books on the observation tower. The tower provided a great view with the whole zoo sprawled out below, but I suspected that Jeremy went there just to be alone!

Jack, in his usual irresponsible way, didn't even offer any help and wandered all around the zoo, climbing onto trees and jumping around screeching like a monkey, often scaring

What the Dreams Whisper

the birds, all the while taking selfies and videos to post on social media. He quickly chummed up with all the zookeepers too. To be honest, I didn't mind that my brothers were not much help because I was enjoying myself.

One day, as I was feeding Polly the macaw, Jack ran up to me, waving and shouting like a maniac. Polly instantly flew away and I shot my brother a warning glare.

"Never mind that!" Jack exclaimed happily. "I just found the most interesting thing ever! Jeremy! Get your nose out of that silly book and come see what I've found!"

He dragged us to the lion's residence, and through the glass wall pointed at an old, gnarled tree inside it. The tree had a few ripe, exotic fruits. They looked juicy, with sunset-colored skin and a pearlike shape. All three of us stared longingly at it. They looked very tasty.

"Kim, the lion-woman says the tree has been here for centuries. The fruits are delicious but Bill decides who gets to eat them! She says you have to 'earn the fruit,' whatever that means," said Jack.

"Well, looks like it is not for us then," said Jeremy wistfully.

"Don't give up so fast, brother!" Jack winked and ran away to continue his shenanigans.

We shook our heads and walked back to resume our duties.

Soon, our last day was here, and I said special goodbyes to each of my bird friends. Finally I climbed up the observation tower to enjoy the sight once more! It was then that I saw a suspicious figure in a bright yellow shirt climbing the wall of the lion's den. It was undoubtedly Jack!

I yelled at him to stop, but he either didn't hear my frantic screams or just ignored them. I quickly scrambled down the tower and started running toward him. Jeremy also ran behind me.

But when we were almost at the corner to the lion's den, we heard something that made my heart leap to my throat.

Jack's familiar voice was yelling, "GET OFF ME RIGHT NOW, YOU BEAST!"

We heard attempts of struggle and a roar. We turned the corner and rushed toward the noise and find Jack…

…restrained by a security guard?!

"LET ME GO!" Jack demanded.

The lion roared again quite nearby on the other side of the wall.

"Lucky for you that we're monitoring everything through security cameras," the security guard grumbled and pushed Jack toward the manager's office.

We followed them. Inside the office we found Grandpa talking with Bill. They looked at us in alarm as the guard recounted what had happened.

"I wanted the fruit that grew in the lion's den, so I thought I would just climb in and quickly get one," Jack mumbled meekly.

Grandpa stared at him in disbelief and anger. "How can you be so irresponsible Jack? Wait until we get back home!"

"I'm s-s-sorry!" Jack stuttered, realizing he was in big trouble.

What the Dreams Whisper

At that moment Bill picked up a bowl and uncovered it with a flourish revealing the very fruit. We gaped at the fruit in awe, and it looked even better close up!

"I thought that maybe this fruit would be a nice thank-you gift for your free service," Bill explained, raising an eyebrow at Jack. He bowed his head in shame.

"This fruit is unique because only special people can enjoy it," he added.

Forgetting his shame, Jack eagerly grabbed it, took one big bite of it, and instantly spat it out.

"Ugh!" Jack said. "This tastes disgusting!"

Jeremy took a tiny nibble of the fruit.

"It's not that bad, but nothing special either" he said, confused.

I cautiously took a bite, but it tasted nothing like they described. A burst of flavor exploded in my mouth. It tasted better than chocolate ice cream, with brownies and whipping cream. It was even better than Grandad's famous chocolate chip cookies with milk.

"This fruit is delicious!" I exclaimed and quickly gobbled it up.

My brothers stared at me in bewilderment.

Bill chuckled, "As I mentioned before, this is a *special* fruit, and its specialty is that it tastes different to each person according to how well they've earned it. The zookeepers call it 'the Fruit of Endurance' as they find it very tasty after a day of hard work!"

We listened to him, fascinated.

"Hardworking average Joes have their special moments too, huh, Joey?" Grandpa asked me with a teasing wink, and I definitely believed him from that moment!

What the Dreams Whisper

Last Gasp

Charlotte Paterson

"What are you reading, Duncan?"

"*Little Women*," he replied. "Why?"

"Well, I was wondering if I may read it after you?" I asked.

"Take it," he said. "I don't really like it anyway."

"And why is that?" I replied.

"Well, I'm at the part where one of them gets scarlet fever and the author just won't get to the point."

There was an uncomfortable silence. Then I sat down on the couch as I watched Duncan leave the living room. It was raining all over Glasgow and I just couldn't wait to get outside again. Anticipatingly, I sat down, excited to start reading.

The book had a lovely leather cover with gold engravings. I flipped through the pages and found where Duncan had left his bookmark. "Hmm," I wondered. I read the first sentence. "'I am not afraid of death, Jo. And I will be homesick for you even in heaven.'"

That must be the one with scarlet fever, I thought.

As I glanced up toward the small table in front of me, I noticed a photo of Duncan. I let out a heaving sigh and yanked it off into my hand. He was wearing nice clothes in front of the church. You could barely recognize him since he has grown so much taller and mature since the photo was taken in 1908. I was only three months from my thirteenth birthday and I still looked younger than I really was.

Suddenly, Mum's hollering voice came from the kitchen downstairs, breaking the silence. "Lilly, come help me with the dinner!"

"Coming, Mum," I responded.

As I walked down the cold wooden stairs, I felt a sudden wave of exhaustion come over me. Then the world seemed to spin a little. Alarmed, I grasped the railing for support. It quickly passed, but it was very peculiar. I hurriedly rushed down the stairs. The glorious aroma of the steak pie wafted through the kitchen.

"Set the table," Mum said as I entered the room.

I nodded. As I went to grab the cutlery, I let out a bitter cough.

"Lilly, are you all right?" Mum cried.

I was not all right, I thought.

She turned to look at me for a moment. "Hmm, well hurry up and set the table then."

We all sat down for a delicious dinner of steak pie and steamed carrots. My family wolfed it down as I just stared blankly at my food.

"Are you all right?" Laurence piped, noticing my odd behavior. "Your skin looks a little blue."

I stared down at my food that now looked unappetizing.

"I don't have an appetite," I replied.

"Lilly, how do you feel?" Mum asked in a small voice.

"My chest hurts, and I have a headache."

"Oh goodness! Go up to your room and I'll call the doctor."

I obediently started toward the hall. I felt dizzy, and before I knew it, the world was spinning, my head hurt twice as bad, and all of a sudden it all went black.

I awoke in my bed beaded with sweat with a stabbing chest pain. A harrowing cough escaped my mouth. Along with the mucus came blood. The red splatted my bedsheets and caused deep stains. Just then Mum rushed in and came to my side. The doctor entered urgently behind her. Another horrific cough arose, this time with yellow mucus instead of blood. The doctor sat me up and took out a strange-looking bottle. He took a spoon and poured the liquid on it. He exigently put the spoon in my mouth and forced me to swallow the liquid. A glass of water followed. Mum darted out of the room and came back a few minutes later with a cold damp towel. Then she sat it on my forehead.

"Will she be all right?" Mum asked concerningly.

"I am afraid she has—" The doctor paused. "Pneumonia," he finished solemnly.

My chest felt as if it were a shield being hit by a sword over and over until I knew it would eventually break. Another cough swelled up at the back of my throat and with it came more blood and more mucus and more pain until all that was left was the dry, scratchy consistency of my mouth.

Mum clung to my arm like an alligator to its prey. She was up on the bed with me now, and I could feel the soft silks of her nightgown on my skin. A warm feeling entered my body and I felt safe. Mum planted a kiss on my head. There were tears in her eyes now. She wrapped her arms around me. I remembered the words of that girl with scarlet fever in *Little Women*.

"'I am not afraid of death, Jo. And I will be homesick for you even in heaven.'"

The room seemed stuffy and the air felt thick. I let out a freakish wheeze. The oxygen was disappearing for my lungs! It felt like everything was being sucked out of me, and I let out one last desperate gasp before my eyes went blurry and in my last moments Mum whispered to me through her tears.

"I love you, Lilly, and will never stop loving you."

Her arms were wrapped snugly around my body. I knew it was my time, and I slowly drifted away to walk among my ancestors in heaven.

What the Dreams Whisper

Get Back Up
Brooklyn Maday

"Freak," Darian whispered into my ear as I walked past him in the hallway.

"Says you," Lidia remarked.

Lidia always came to my defense. Since kindergarten, we have been friends.

I have social anxiety so when I arrived in the classroom the first time I was overwhelmed and too afraid to make friends. Luckily, Lidia did all the talking so it was easy to get along, and it was easy to stay in my own little bubble.

Lidia has a rare skin condition called vitiligo. This causes her to have rough white patches all over her perfect caramel skin. I am an albino girl. My parents both carried the albinism gene, and although they knew this, they were still quite surprised that I turned out to be an albino.

Lidia always said that we pair perfectly together because we are both unique and beautiful. I disagreed. I mean she was gorgeous, but I was a freak and I always would be.

"Thanks," I murmured under my breath.

Whispers filled the hallway as we continued to walk arm in arm to math class. I took a peek at Lidia, her head held high in the air and her confidence radiating from her warm chestnut eyes to her wide dimpled smile. I looked down at my hands, which were twitching nervously.

"Ugh, look at the two freaks," I heard a ginger boy whisper.

I thought Lidia was going to get upset, but she just kept her head up high.

Every day was pretty much the same thing. I get teased, she stands up for me, I get kicked, she kicks them back, and on and on. I always wished I could be like her, have confidence, and be strong. Instead I am just the albino girl who keeps her head down and takes all the blows.

"How was your day?" my mom asked as I entered the door to our house that afternoon.

"Good."

Lidia was always telling me that I took my parents for granted and how she wished she had parents that would greet her when she got home, would kiss her good night, and walk her to school. I've only seen her confidence break once, and that was when she would talk about her parents.

"HEY," Lidia called the next morning. "Wait up!"

"Morning," I mumbled to Lidia as we walked up to the school.

Lidia babbled on and on for a while like she always does while we walk to class.

The next day was the same as every day, and so was the next, and then the next, and so on. Until one day I arrived at school and Lidia wasn't there.

"Where's Lidia?" I asked the girl Emma who sat next to me.

"How would I know?" she responded. "I don't talk to freaks like her. Which reminds me I shouldn't be talking to a freak like you."

Pretty much all the conversations that I have tried to start end like that.

About a week passed, and Lidia still wasn't showing up for school. Although it seemed like no one even knew she was missing. I mainly kept to myself and tried not to talk to anyone, but Darian still noticed me and bullied me every day. The only difference about his bullying was that now I had no one to encourage me to be myself and stand up for me.

Another week passed, and anxiety was the only emotion I could feel. Questions ran through my head like "Where is Lidia?" or "Why isn't Lidia at school?" or even "Is she hurt or worse dead?" I tried not to think about the last one, but sometimes in the dead of night when I couldn't sleep that was all I could think about.

The next Monday I arrived at school and there was Lidia!

"OMG, I missed you so much," I exclaimed. "Where the heck were you?!"

"Oh, well, uh—"

The ring of the bell cut her off. Although, I couldn't help but notice the worried look on her face.

We went through all our classes and were on the way to lunch when Darian cut us off like he always did. I was prepared for Lidia to tell him to "MOVE!" but when I looked at her, her head was down staring at her feet.

"Hey, freaks. Where have you been, Lidia? It's been quite a while since I've seen your ugly face," Darian sneered.

Lidia's eyes were still on her feet.

"OOOO! Someone's scared. What are you scared of? Never mind, I know. Jake lives next to you and he told me that your old man has been beating you. He heard your screams from across the street," he sneered.

I couldn't help but let a little gasp escape my lips. What was going on?

"Oh your little freak friend here doesn't know the story, does she?" he said. "Hmm, it doesn't seem like you're gonna spit it out, so how about I tell her? How does that sound freak? Well, for your information, Lidia's father beats her so her mom decided to take Lidia away last week, but when she realized that she didn't have enough money to support them, she came crawling back to her husband."

A sob escaped Lidia's lips, and I looked over at her to see a little tear fall down her perfectly imperfect face. Yet still I expected her to come back with a snappy comment like she always did.

"Aw, poor little crybaby. Does she need her mommy? Oh wait, her mommy is gone."

I looked up with a confused expression.

"Oh yeah, I forgot to add that. After her mom dropped her off with her dad, she took off."

Another sob out of Lidia. I watched her shoulders shake and droop like a million-pound weight was on them. As I watched tear after tear slip down her cheeks leaving a wet streak, I felt anger fuel inside me. Who did he think he was making fun of my best friend like that? WHO?! I thought of all the times Lidia had encouraged me to stand up for myself, all the times she had told me that I was enough to brighten someone's world up, all the times she told me that I was a gorgeous girl, all the times *she* had stood up for me.

"Well, you know what, Darian? She isn't going to live with her dad—she is going to live with my family and me! She won't have to deal with someone beating her like she did for the last twelve years. And you also know what? At least she has someone like me to love her and be her sister," I screamed in his ugly, ugly face. "Now get out of our way so that we can get our lunch and talk about how we are going to decorate our room!" I punched him in the face so hard he began to cry, but I didn't care! He could die for all I cared. I shoved through him, dragging a still sobbing Lidia with me.

"C'mon," I mumbled to Lidia as I took her to our regular table.

I left her to grab our lunches, and when I came back, she was done crying and was left with bloodshot eyes and a puffy face.

"Are you okay?" I asked gently. The anger in me had started to wear off and I was just waiting for the anxiety attack to kick in, but surprisingly I wasn't anxious. I was proud, I was confident, and I was who I always wanted to be.

Lidia nodded, then opened her mouth to speak but instead of her normal bright voice it came out as a croaky rasp.

"Hey, don't worry about talking," I said. "You're seriously good. We can talk about it later. Just relax right now, okay?" I waited for Lidia to nod.

The rest of the day passed, and we were just about to leave school when I decided that I wasn't going to let Lidia go home to her father.

"Lidia," I called, "come with me okay. Here, take my hand."

Together we walked to my house hand in hand.

Epilogue

"Sarahhhhhh!" Lidia called. "Wake up!"

"What?" I responded groggily.

"It's time to get ready for school!"

My parents had agreed to try to get custody of Lidia. They had called CPS to talk about her father and mother and try to come up with a solution so that somehow we could get Lidia.

Lidia's father wanted nothing to do with her, and her mother was currently trying to get back on her feet, so they both agreed that my parents could have full custody.

I got my outfit, which was a pair of leggings, a light purple shirt, and Converse, and we left the house.

Classes were as usual except that day, like every day the past two months, Darian didn't bully me, I was able to talk to people besides Lidia, and I now had a whole group of friends.

And now I knew that even if I got bullied or someone was a jerk to me, I *would* be able to stand up for myself. And if someone pushed me down, I *would* get back up.

The Book Catastrophe
Tommy Liu

Screech!

Oh sorry, Kenji here. My brother made me record this and…*slice.* Phew, that was a close one. Where was I? Oh yes—I'm currently trying to defeat a ten-foot tall scorpion with advanced shielding.

One day I'm living very comfortably; the next day I'm fleeing for my life…

***

Egypt was once a colorless country until the day it suddenly exploded in colors.

Unfortunately, this was not necessarily good; it was an unnatural disaster, because Egypt was currently being bombarded by books falling from the sky!

"Do you happen to know what in the world is happening?" I asked my mother just after I had finished my morning routine.

I could tell she was concerned, but she didn't want to talk about it. When I asked her, she said she had to get something done. As she left, my two brothers entered the kitchen behind her.

"What was that about?" questioned Storm, my older brother who thought he was more SUPERIOR than myself. Hence why he made me do things for him, such as THIS written record for apparently no reason.

"I don't want to talk about it," I answered hesitantly.

"It appears that someone who has been very talkative has finally stopped speaking!" exclaimed my younger, annoying little brother, Rush, who always rushed into things.

"What are *you* doing here?" I said, but before my little brother could say a word, we were interrupted.

"Fine," said Storm, "I'm wondering how in the world there are books falling from the sky, and don't you dare bore me to death because I'm sick of it."

I tried to be helpful. "Do you need medicine? Because I think you said you're sick, and let me see, I'm going to need a few ingredients, so I need the…"

"That's not the point, brother, because…wait, did you even hear my question?" Storm questioned.

"Wait, are you trying to provoke me with an invisible sword or a sharp and extremely thin needle because I don't see one?" I said, confused.

"Ugh," Storm said under his breath. "I will figure it out myself."

And with that, he stormed away.

"Umm, he was trying to ask you why there are books falling from the sky," exclaimed Rush.

"How should I know? Go ask our father, the king of the pharaohs," I responded.

"Okay, I agree," replied Rush.

Unable to stop my own curiosity, including my confusion as to why my mother wouldn't engage in a conversation, I followed my little brother.

When we got to the king, Storm was already there.

"You're early, for once," Storm said annoyingly.

"Enough," boomed the king. "This is a catastrophe. I can't even go outside in this weather. I have no idea which of my enemies have done this. You must consult the Oracle!"

"Why, Dad?!" I complained. "I can't go with them; they'll mess up or even get lost!"

But the king just said, "Go with them or don't go at all."

Well, that settled it, and me and my annoying brothers ran to the Oracle. (Because of Rush, ugh.)

Anyways, before we went, we secured some armor as protection so we wouldn't become pancakes! And off we went to the Oracle's temple located at the very tip of a green mountain.

"Oh, Oracle, what should we do to save our country from this destruction?" Storm was the first of us to speak on account of being the eldest. He averted his eyes out of respect, and we also held our eyes down toward the ground.

The Oracle, a mythical mummy, sat on a three-legged stool. Before she would help us, we would have to make an offering, so I threw in some half-baked sand cookies and said, "Hope you like the cookies because the main ingredient, sand, is difficult to find because of the books now covering the sand. They are all lying down against each other."

The Oracle opened her mouth, and the words that came out floated around the temple like music:

"To save your country from disaster

You must act faster,

To go on the hero's path,

And calm Throth's wrath.

To return the book that tells,

And to make Throth well.

To defeat a forgotten enemy,

Then you will reveal your identity."

And with that, the Oracle closed her mouth and her eyes, and she went, as if, back to sleep. She had given us, *apparently*, all we needed.

My brothers looked at me with true confusion.

"I don't get it either," I said.

"I think the Oracle wants us to go on a quest," said Rush slowly.

And before Storm or I could follow that up, Rush was on his way out.

"What are you fools waiting for? Let's go!"

***

And so you are now up to speed with why I am currently in the predicament that I am in.

SWOOSH!

Like I said, if I was about to die over here, I was going to blame it on Rush.

SLICE, HISS.

Because he rushed off somewhere, then we had to follow him, and that led all of us into a trap, straight into this particular scorpion's den. Let's just say it took a lot of banana peels until the demon slipped, giving us an opportunity to shimmy past him. We were in the lair of the scorpion, but it was so vast, we found ourselves lost many times, but we…no…I tied a string in the beginning so that we could all get back out. Again, an indication of how much my brothers needed me.

The walls here contained evil, and the smell of rotten eggs lurked from every corner.

"Ew," I said in disgust.

Then a deep and booming voice said, "Maw-hahaha, my plan is almost complete. 'When that bird realizes his mistake, it would be too late but...'" The voice paused. "The last part of the inscription is missing from the book," the voice groaned. "I thought I was one step ahead of those brats, with the book that knows everything!"

"That creature of evil has the book!" I whispered.

"Yeah, we all know that. Brilliant observation. How do we steal it?" mocked Storm.

Before I could respond, Rush ran toward the evil creature, who turned out to be a serpent, and chirped: "Hi, can we please have the book?"

Then the serpent lunged, but Rush was too fast and escaped from his claws, running to the temple of Throth...wait, did I mention that it had claws? Because it did.

Anyways, at the temple of Throth, Storm joked, "I wonder what this birdbrain will say. He might say, 'How dare you enter my temple; you'll die now!'"

Suddenly, there was a booming voice "I'm Throth! How dare you enter my temple; you'll die now! Ohhh, never mind. You're the kids of the maiden I was supposed to protect—Aset, who you may know as Isis! You can search it up online."

"What do you mean by *online*?" I asked curiously.

"It's, er, forget it," Throth answered. "Why are you here in the first place?"

"To stop this giant serpent who took your book," Storm answered.

Throth thought about this for a moment and then encouraged us to explain our journey. Several minutes ticked by, and we finally finished our story.

"I see," Throth said, smiling. "I can tell you how to finish your quest. Here are the last lines of the prophecy."

Throth pulled out a piece of parchment that had the remaining prophetic lines waiting for them: "But magic would save the day, and for the evil's delay."

"Now let's go trap a serpent," said Throth, looking very optimistic.

Under his protection, the boys were kept safe from the falling books as they proceeded toward the serpent's den.

"Where are those pesky mammals?" hissed the serpent furiously.

"I'm over here," screamed Rush, running in one direction.

"I'm over here," screamed Storm, running in another direction.

"But what about me? I'm over here!" I screamed, hopping toward the rocks.

The serpent grabbed me and my brothers using his tail and claws, but little did he know, things were going according to *our* plan, not his.

"That was too easy," cracked the serpent.

"You have not won!" shouted Throth.

"What are you doing here? "asked the serpent. "I can take on one god."

"That's your mistake," said Throth, laughing. "Tip number one: don't tell your enemy your weakness."

"WHAT?" screamed the serpent.

Throth then revealed that Aset was with him.

"Now," roared Throth.

Aset then muttered a few words, and vines erupted from the floor, sending the serpent deep into the ground. The magic resounded in the cave, but left me and my brothers, and of course the Book of Knowledge (I mean, that was the point of all this, right?) perfectly safe.

Throth, now pacified and happy to have his precious book back, stopped the unnatural disaster that was plaguing Egypt. With a sudden boom, the books all stopped raining down and disappeared entirely from the ground.

My brothers and I returned home after our incredible journey. Our father, who had aged considerably throughout this crisis, gave his crown to Storm and left the kingdom under his rule. Rush, you guessed it, competed (and won, boring) the first Olympics.

And me? I became a writer, documenting our journeys and the history of Egypt. Though we aren't together anymore, I often get many letters from my bothers...*ding dong*. Time to return this recorded history to my brother King Storm whose servant has now arrived to retrieve it. Aset and Throth, well, let's just say they went back to their godly business...

A Dagger from the Past
Leonard Chong

I looked out my cable car window at a sleeping giant, cradling me with its great white arms. The alpine air filled my lungs. My car ticked gently up the mountain to a plateau that was suspended midair. I'd spent the day skiing. Before the day ended, I would meet an old hippie. Wind battered against my face like sharp blades, and waves of cold washed over me like a blanket.

The door of the inn slammed open as I barged inside, expecting to see a well-dressed man waiting for me. Instead, the sight that greeted my eyes was shocking. In the corner of the entrance hall, on a velvet cushion chair, sat the messiest looking old man I have ever seen in my entire lifetime. A few strands of gray hair hung down over his gold-spectacled, almond eyes. The twelve pockets of his cashmere cardigan were stuffed with papers. We were the only guests in the inn. He looked friendly. We agreed to grab a hot chocolate.

Leaning across the mahogany table in the coffee house, he introduced himself as Joe Piper. He took a little bottle out of his cardigan, which was filled with what looked like golden powder. "Nanomachines."

I raised an eyebrow.

He then patiently explained to me that his machines could play with space and time. "If you don't trust me," whispered the scientist, "you can try it."

The scientist swiftly dropped some gold into my drink.

Instinctively, I sipped it. The chocolate was delicious, after all.

But dizziness overcame me. My legs seemed to crumble.

Gradually, a silvery mist swallowed me up, and the bar receded into nothingness—

But then, I felt my legs again and stumbled forward, seeking ground.

Ahead of me, a building—a concrete monstrosity, like the prow of a ship in a storm—took form. Its faceless walls glared down at me, topped with barbed wire, like rings of ugly crowns.

I was alone.

Deserted on this island.

And I remembered, from a photo, what this place was.

Abruptly, invisible hands seemed to grab me and lift me up into the air, out of the silky mist. I gasped for breath, wriggling to try and get free, but the hands held on in tight coils, tightening and tightening. The bar, welcome in its red-and-gold comfort, returned, and I felt hard wood on my back. For once in my life, I felt elated to be lying on the floor of a bar.

Regaining my balance and massaging my throat, I interrogated my kindly new friend, who took his hands off my shoulder and sat quietly.

"Alcatraz…that wasn't…just a drug. That vision was too swift. Too solid. And why there?"

A shrug.

"I live in the Bay Area, on the mainland just east of it, so it just jumped into my mind."

He eyed me curiously and continued.

"Young man, I am selling this item for a few rounds of time travel. I was a former scientist, now retired. Would you like to go for a round with these magnificent machines...perhaps to fix a problem in your past?"

I still wasn't sure if I drank "machines," but I had to feel it again. I slapped a wad of cash onto the table.

A gleam appeared in Piper's eyes as he stared greedily at the money. He nodded.

He handed me the entire bottle of golden powder. After I finally finished the last of the golden powder, I thought I saw a crooked grin stretch across his face before I disappeared into the unknown.

Instead of finding the time before my dad's death, I found myself back in front of Alcatraz prison.

***

I stood back flat against the cool stone wall in the darkness. Out of the blue, I felt a shadow creep up on me behind my back, sending shivers up my spine like a snake slowly slithering toward its prey.

"Boy! Whaddya think you're doin' in my cell?" yelled a voice that sent me jumping at least a meter into the air.

"Who are you?" I squeaked concerningly like a mouse.

"Al Capone," said the person calmly.

He had a gravelly voice, which seemed to quake my eardrums with every word he spoke.

"People call me Scarface."

He walked up to me and I immediately realized why they called him that. His face was covered in battle scars. He was also short and on the round side.

His battle-scarred face was now pensive, however, and he then said the strangest thing I'd expect to hear on my journey.

"Let's make a deal. The only way out of this prison is by leaving a distraction when guards check on our cell every night; that gives you time to get out. This place is full of maintenance tunnels; with a bit of time, you can cut to them and run —then sail. A fellow like you is a good distraction. I call the shots around here; I can get you paid."

I scrunched up a menacing expression, trying to look as fierce as possible. Making my voice deep and metallic, I mumbled, "Deal, Capone."

At exactly seven that night, a typical guard walked past the prison cells. He was bored and feeling unwell, down in the dumps. Nothing interesting happens on patrol duty. The best he could do to entertain himself was to sneer and say extremely insulting sentences to the inmates.

Today, he was handing out supper to all of them. Entering the cell Al Capone shared with another inmate who he didn't even know the name of, he saw Scarface (as all of the prison guards called him too) lying in his bed sleeping like a gorilla.

The guard flung the bowl of food unceremoniously onto the floor and walked out of the prison cell. Tried to.

Everything seemed to happen in one exact second.

The air vent on top of the prison cell fell open.

Al Capone 2.0 dropped out of it and landed on the guard.

The guard was knocked out cold.

Al Capone and Al Capone 2.0 ran out of the cell as quickly as they possibly could out of one of the old maintenance tunnels.

Ripping off a face mask that exactly resembled Al Capone's face (made by one of his cronies), I ran out onto the hard, golden brown sand as we searched for a raft or anything that could float on water. Eventually Al Capone found a tree and barged into it, knocking it over with his inhumane strength. Then he flipped the tree over and put it on the shore, telling me to get on as quickly as I can possibly manage. Next, with one mighty shove of his hands, we were out in the mysterious depths of the sea.

A few hours later, they saw a glint of scintillating light shimmering from somewhere not far away. Suddenly, with a swift flick of his hand, Al Capone knocked the breath out of me, and I dropped like a stone into the deep sea below.

***

Days later, I was awakened by the rising tide on a mainland beach.

I suppressed my anger at Capone. He was a criminal and acted like one; trusting him was just my mistake. I kicked sand off my prison clothes and crept up to a little house by the beach, a car sleeping in a garage by its side.

As I thought about this, a surge of scarlet fury rushed to my head. Everything that had happened was caused by one person—that old hippie, Joe Piper.

This person was the cause of me not seeing my family and friends again.

The cause of me ending up in Alcatraz.

The cause of me getting knocked out by Capone.

I had a plan.

I reached the home and saw a lonely figure walk up to it.

A person whose features resembled Joe Piper, only younger. Creeping up behind him, I trailed this wicked person through sun-drenched French doors.

After slipping into his house after him, I finally showed myself by yelling, "Joe!"

The good scientist jumped and turned around slowly.

"How do you know my name?" he whimpered.

"I just do. Now, Joe, use your time machine and send me forward in time now!"

His head gave a sad little shake. "I'm sorry. I don't know how to do that."

Dread washed over me like ice-cold water.

I could never go home.

This man, standing here, was pretending to be innocent.

I roared like a beast and leaped onto the man, my vision red with rage.

A few minutes later, I returned to consciousness and saw my red, shivering hands. Looking down at the floor, I saw a body lying there, the body of Joe Piper. A pool of blood silently spread out on the floor beneath him. I killed the man who was my only hope of returning to my time. Sick with the taste of metal in the air, I screamed.

***

Four hours later, the police found two men lying dead on the floor. An inmate and…a scientist.

***

Miles away, Joe Piper sipped his coffee, staring out of the window. A briefcase glowed in the chandelier light by his feet. He would be rich! Richer than in his dreams!

But a sharp, stabbing pain shot up Piper's chest and neck, as if his cells were being torn apart.

He collapsed by the case, which sat as if staring beatifically, unused. Little by little, as Joe lay twitching on the floor, his body faded. The last thing he saw were his bleeding eyes reflected in the briefcase's golden lock.

This Should Not Be Scary

Amber Chiao

The day was warm and bright; there were barely any clouds in the sky. No one would think this a terrifying time of day, but Quinn was shivering. He didn't care what time it was; every step he took was full of fear. He clutched his backpack straps tighter. In his mind, every stranger around him might be a blood-sucking beast, ready to swoop down on him and drain him dry. Ever since vampires had become accustomed to sunlight, the streets were swarming with them, at least according to Quinn. Technically it was illegal for vampires to feed before sundown, but that didn't stop Quinn from being his usual jumpy self.

Vampires, elves, and humans, all of them on the same planet, miraculously living in… somewhat of a harmony. They all had a similar, unearthly quality that made Quinn really nervous. The vampires had silver-tinged hair and required blood once a week to not go "feral." If they did go feral, they would be blinded by a lust for blood and would kill for it. Elves had pointed ears and hair color ranging from pink to green. With hands capable of healing small injuries, they were the most peaceful and emotional species.

Quinn was mostly scared of vampires. Elves were still powerful, of course, but it wasn't like they drank human blood. However, both of these species went to his school, so he had isolated himself out of fear. He had done a pretty good job of it too, considering he now had only one friend he felt he could trust.

Continuing on his walk to school, Quinn felt a tug on his backpack; it was his best and only friend, Jonas.

"You almost gave me a heart attack!" Quinn glared at Jonas, momentarily letting go of his backpack straps.

"*Everything* gives you a heart attack. Also, we have a new kid today. He's my cousin from overseas so I've gotta get to school as soon as possible." When Jonas spoke, he gestured at the air very comically, as if he was conducting an orchestra.

"I don't care. I don't ne—" Before he could finish his sentence about "not needing more friends" Jonas had already started dragging Jonas toward the school.

A wave of cold air-conditioned air hit the two boys' faces as they entered. A pink-haired boy smiled at them from across the room and raised a hand in a greeting.

He has pink hair, and sharp ears...he's an elf! Quinn thought. *Is Jonas an elf too?* He shook his head to clear out this thought; Jonas had brown hair and hazel eyes, and his ears weren't pointed. Nothing about Jonas fit the "elf" category.

"Are you okay?" The sound of the voice of the newcomer brought Quinn back to reality.

Jonas shook his head. "He's fine. He always does that, just spaces out. I'm guessing he was on Mars."

Quinn held a hand toward Jonas's cousin, ignoring Jonas's comment. "I'm Quinn, nice to meet you."

The other boy shook his hand, grinning cheerfully. "You can call me Thomas!" Thomas seemed to have the same friendly energy as Jonas.

The school day passed like a breeze. As usual Quinn tried hard in all the subjects but still only managed to get a C in math. Jonas slapped him on the back. "Highest you've ever gotten!" he teased.

Quinn pushed Jonas's hand away. "Good job getting a C- in English!" he said back sarcastically.

"I can help you guys!" Thomas spoke up. "Just come over to my house, and I'll get you both straightened out!"

They agreed and headed toward Thomas's house.

As they entered Thomas's room, the curtains were closed. In the dark, Quinn noticed Thomas's eyes. They seemed to be glowing! He stepped back warily. "What...what *are* you?!"

Thomas smiled, his eyes still blue, but shining like LED lights in the dark. "Vampire-elf hybrid, nice to meet you."

Jonas stared at Thomas frantically. "But y-you...since when?!"

Thomas held his hands in the air. "I'm not here to take your blood. I genuinely just want to help out the two of you."

The two boys were fearful of Thomas the entire time they worked, and eye contact was completely out of the question. They always made sure there was a fair amount of distance between them, and they had a way to make a quick escape, whether it was through the door or the window. Finally, they were done. As the two boys hurried to pack their things, Thomas's mother walked in.

Her hair was silver and she carried a few Ziplock bags of blood. "Thomas, don't forget your weekly supply!"

Thomas leaped up and tore the bag open. The crimson liquid leaked out and flowed onto his fingers, leaving a red trail behind. He drank the blood, closing his eyes as he guzzled. Thomas finally opened his eyes once he had finished and the other two were staring at him, flabbergasted and disgusted.

"We need to go…" Jonas said, a note of panic in his voice. He grabbed Quinn's arm, and the two bolted out of the house, not stopping until they reached their own.

Thomas stared at the two leaving, noticing how frightened and disgusted they seemed of him. Almost as if…as if he was a monster. He blinked hard to hold back the tears. He wanted to call after them, but he couldn't. His legs seemed glued to the ground and his mouth seemed blocked. He was heartbroken, especially by his own cousin.

Thomas's mother simply sighed and placed a hand on her son's shoulder.

During the next day at school, Jonas and Quinn avoided Thomas, not even offering a simple greeting. Thomas felt unwanted. Jonas and Quinn were the only people he had talked to on his first day, and he was much too shy to go up to any other student, so he sat alone all day in a puddle of misery.

Not wanting to stay this way forever, Thomas decided to go up to the pair after school and confront them. But before he could work up the courage, they had already begun walking toward him.

"Thomas?" Jonas asked softly. "Sorry about yesterday…for just leaving you like that."

Quinn was scared of vampires, but Thomas seemed to be friendly.

"It was rude, and we're sorry," Quinn said, looking Thomas in the eye.

Thomas forgave them and all seemed to be well. The three boys hung out together and helped each other out on their studies.

Then one day, when the trio were on the school playground, Thomas's arm began to tremble. Jonas looked over. "Thomas, why are your eyes purple…?"

Thomas's incisors were longer than average and extremely sharp. His eyes turned a bright red, and with a cry, he tackled Jonas to the ground.

Quinn struggled to get Thomas off Jonas. It was like he suddenly had gained super strength and was clinging onto Jonas. When he finally succeeded, Thomas set his sights on Quinn and began attacking him instead.

All the other students were watching them. Quinn started to run, hoping to lure Thomas away from Jonas, but Thomas was smarter than that. He headed toward Jonas who was backing away slowly. "Thomas…listen, buddy…"

Quinn pounced onto Thomas, pinning him onto the ground with his hands behind his back. Thomas looked back at Quinn with his red eyes. "Blood…human…"

Sticking his arm in front of Thomas's face, Quinn let him go slightly. "Will this do…?"

He was terrified, but Thomas seemed to be feral and would most likely harm everyone else present if it meant getting the blood he needed, so just giving it to him now seemed to be the best option.

Thomas didn't even hesitate. He sank his incisors deep into his skin, and small drops of crimson blood oozed out where he bit. Quinn winced slightly, but it wasn't as bad as he anticipated. It was slightly sore, but the excruciating pain that he expected never came.

His eyes turned purple, then back to blue. His incisors retracted and he looked at Quinn. "W-what happened...?"

"You went feral..." Quinn was busy staring at where Thomas had bit down. Where he expected there to be two gaping holes, there was smooth skin, completely unharmed. He drew his attention back to Thomas. "When was the last time you had blood?"

"Since the time you both came over...four weeks ago." Thomas looked up at Quinn sheepishly.

"*What?!*" Jonas looked at Thomas in absolute disbelief, not knowing whether to be angry or sympathetic. "Don't vampires need blood every week or something?"

"Also, I got bit by you—am I a vampire now?" This was the only question Quinn cared about at that point.

"Yes, yes, we do. And, Quinn, no, you're not a vampire. I would need to bite your neck, and you would need a full vampire's blood in your system. I'm only half."

Quinn was relieved. Jonas was not. "WHY WOULD YOU NOT—"

"I tried to stop drinking blood and maybe just rely on my elf side, because I was scared you guys would ignore me again if I continued my vampire ways and—"

"Not a chance," Quinn said firmly, interrupting him.

Thomas's face was full of relief. He smiled and smiled.

The day was warm and bright; there were close to no clouds in the sky. It looked like it was a beautiful day for everyone.

The Myth of Medusa
Madelyn Wong Hei Ching

The stone statue of Medusa stood at the corner of the Metropolitan Museum of Art, waiting for the right one to finally wake her up. She had been deep asleep for thousands of years. If only someone would read out those magic words to break her curse.

If you have heard of the myth of Medusa, let me assure you that the story is real. However, she wasn't defeated by cutting off her head, but by using a mirror to reflect her gaze and turned herself into stone. Now, her statue was in the Metropolitan Museum of Art. She needed someone to speak the magic words so she could be free.

One day, a man in black cloak walked to the statue. The other visitors all looked at him curiously. He looked straight to the statue's eyes and muttered, "Medusa, let your eyes be free of your own power. Curse breakasum!"

The moment he finished the sentence, the statue came to life. Her snake-hair hissed as if eager to turn everyone into stone. Medusa looked at the man and nodded to thank him. She then roared and chased after all the petrified people. Some couldn't even say anything before they were turned into stone statues. Some knew what happened and clapped their hands over their eyes just in time. Soon, the museum was full of stone statues.

As soon as Medusa went out of the museum, the outside was filled with scared people too. Everyone knew that looking at Medusa's eyes would turn them to stone, so now everyone covered their eyes no matter what they heard. Some tried to run away but still failed to escape the fate of being turned into stone. As more people were turned into stone statues, Medusa grew stronger and larger. When the people around her all turned into stone, Medusa was already twelve feet tall.

Soon enough, the government heard about the terror of the city.

"General, almost half of the citizens have been turned into stone. What should we do? It won't work if we evacuate the city. We can't move or Medusa will hear us. If this continues, every single person in the city will be turned into stone! We can't let it happen!" a soldier said.

The general knitted his eyebrows and said, 'Warn everyone we can contact and ask the neighboring cities, no, countries for help. We need all the support we can get!"

The soldier saluted and ran to tell the news.

At the same time, the chief secretary dialed the neighboring country's president. "We will get all the soldiers in our country and go to your city as fast as we can. I will also try to ask for help from other countries. Don't worry."

The president immediately gathered every soldier and ordered them to prepare for a battle.

Not long after, a swarm of tanks rushed into the city and started to fire guns at Medusa. She roared in rage and turned a tank upside down. The people in the tank ran out and started using their smaller guns to hit Medusa. However, she only had to swipe her hand and half of the tanks flipped around. Some soldiers accidently looked her in the eye and were turned into stone in a flash. More tanks were defeated, but more tanks were on their way to help, as well as about a dozen helicopters gliding in the sky. As more and more guns were aiming at Medusa, her power seemed to be draining. Finally, her energy was used to its limits and Medusa fell to the ground. She lay still on the ground silently. Some brave soldiers walked slowly to Medusa's body and poked it. She didn't react or move and the stone statues were starting to turn back into humans. People all cheered and yelled, "Yay! She's dead!" They had just defeated a nonhuman creature that was almost undefeatable.

When everyone was busy celebrating, Medusa's snake-hair twitched. A soldier noticed this, but just before he could warn everyone, Medusa stood on her feet and turned some people into stone again. The place turned instantly from delight to shock and fear.

"How did she survive? I thought she died!" the general exclaimed.

"It seems that she just passed out. Now that she's awake, we will have to think of a way to entirely finish her and we have to make sure she won't come back to fight against us again!" a captain from another country said.

"Sir? Sir?"

"Who's there? Show yourself!"

Everyone looked around alarmingly but saw no one.

"Sir, down here."

Everyone looked down and saw a little boy, not older than ten, standing with his head held high to look at the adults. "

What are you doing here, child? How did you even get in here?"

The little boy, without the slightest look of fear or guilt, replied, "I am Mike, sir. I followed you all to get here, but the

What the Dreams Whisper

guards outside didn't seem to see me. I'm here because I found a way to defeat the giant Medusa! Remember the…"

The general raised his hand to stop the boy from jabbering. "How would you, a little boy, defeat the powerful Medusa? You want to be the hero and save everyone, but that won't happen. Go home to your parents and leave it to us."

"B-but, sir…" Mike muttered, but he saw the disbelief in everyone's eyes and lowered his head. He went out of the building and ran home.

"I will do it! I will think of a way to stop her without the army! I will show them I'm not just a little kid!" he said to himself. He stood up and left his house again after he grabbed his dad's motorbike helmet.

The captain was looking down at the war on the ground when he saw a small figure moving closer to Medusa. He squinted and found Mike wearing a helmet, running toward the fighting tanks and Medusa.

"General! Look! The boy who came in here earlier is heading for Medusa! What should we do? He might be hurt by the guns!"

The general rushed to the window and growled, "I should have kept him here to watch him. Now, the only things we can do are stop firing and try to save Mike from Medusa. Order the men to stop firing and try to stop the boy from going any farther!"

Mike dodged and ducked the people that tried to catch him.

"Hey, Medusa! Try and catch me if you can!" the boy shouted at Medusa.

Medusa wheeled around and hissed at the boy. The boy started to run as fast as he could toward a place that would defeat Medusa—the Mirror House. The New York government had built a house with mirrors recently, and Mike wanted to make Medusa look at her own eyes like the last time she was defeated.

Medusa didn't notice where she was heading; she was focused on Mike. She was determined to catch her victim and turn him into a stone statue like the other humans did.

Mike ran as fast as a professional racer, and before long, the boy, along with Medusa behind him, had arrived at the front door of the Mirror House. The tanks that were racing behind came as well, and the people in the tanks held their breaths, waiting for something to happen.

"Hey! I'm in front of you!"

Medusa looked up and stared at the mirror surface of the Mirror House. She seemed dazed when she looked at the mirror.

For a second, Mike wondered if his plan would work or if Medusa would just find Mike and turn him into stone.

Then Medusa wailed as her body transformed into stone. In the blink of an eye, she was a stone statue again. The people that were stone started turning back into normal, and they all looked joyfully at their hero—Mike. They went wild and picked up the boy and lifted him into the air.

The general went up to the celebrating people and signaled them to quiet down.

"I must say, Mike here has saved us all from a horrible disaster. I am so sorry that I misjudged you and said that you couldn't be the hero. Actually everyone can be the hero! Every child, man, woman, and elderly person is able to save the world. Let us now start a celebration party for our young hero!"

Mike walked to the general and said, "I suggest we break the Medusa into pieces, so she won't come back to life again."

The General gave him a big smile and a thumbs-up.

Mike grinned back and joined the crowd. The celebration went on for days.

The world had returned to normal again, and the experience had taught the general an important lesson—don't judge a book by its cover.

About Lune Spark Books

Lune Spark Books aims to encourage children to engage in creating writing. We work with parents and young writers to promote creative fiction writing to help identify talent. We run annual competitions and creative writing classes and publish short stories by the young writers. For more details, visit us at http://youngwriterscontest.com/

Follow us on social media to keep up with the latest updates:
https://www.facebook.com/youngwriterscontest/
https://twitter.com/LuneSparkLLC

Other Anthologies by Lune Spark

A Window to Young Minds

Speaking Up for Each Other

The Emotional Embodiment of Stars

Stained Glass Myths

Just One More

Through Their Lenses

Seasons of Grief

A Few Drops of Hope

Behind Life's Curtain

Written from the Stars

What the Dreams Whisper

Made in the USA
Las Vegas, NV
20 January 2023

65986629R00111